# Defying the Odds

C. L. Kraemer

Published by Rogue Phoenix Press, LLP
Copyright © 2020

ISBN: 978-1-62420-536-1

Cover Art: Designs by Ms. G

# Chapter One

*In a meadow east of Eugene, Oregon*

Bram ambled up the roughly hewn stairs to the willow lounge chair located at the front of his home. He pulled the scrimshawed pipe from his pocket and filled the bowl with his favorite blend of black cherry tobacco. The paced routine of loading the ivory bowl with fragrant leaves and tamping them firmly into place was one of his favorite after dinner rituals. Withdrawing a matchstick from the inner pocket of his vest, he struck the sulfured end against a river rock he'd placed on the root of the towering oak that served as his home.

The fading evening sky showered the mountains in hues of gold and red. Pushing away the light, a blanket of dark blue velvet sprinkled with luminous star points soon prevailed. Bram puffed smoke rings at the darkening heavens.

"Evenin'." A scruffy black and tan terrier mix meandered up and, after circling three times, lay next to the chubby gnome.

"Evening, Silas. How's the family?"

"Well, thank you. Daisy announced we're expecting--again."

Bram chuckled into his beard. "Congratulations."

"Humph. I'll be glad when we're both too old to care. I came over to ask if there are any jobs in sight. I'll need to be working as much as I can now."

It seemed he got one batch of kids out of the house and another was on the way.

Silence stretched between the business partners. Bram pulled deep draughts on his pipe, blowing the smoke away from his friend. His eyes were drawn to the large block of light spilling from the picture window of the behemoth on the hill. The Saun clan, night elves whose callous actions nearly destroyed the fae population of the meadow and surrounding forests, owned the out of place monstrosity.

Bram squinted his eyes to focus his vision on the methodical movement that broke the beam of light. He could just make out a figure pacing rhythmically in front of the casement. Unable to ascertain which of the night elves was engaged in the determined striding, Bram was sure of only one thing…if the night elves were restless and unhappy, the rest of the valley was in trouble.

~ * ~

Gitty paced in front of the picture window, ignoring the expansive view of the green valley below. The thick carpet covering the hand selected hardwood floors muffled the angry stompings of her boots. At the end of each turn, she jabbed the air with her finger.

"Think you can take away my magic, do you?" She spun on the ball of her foot and stamped to the other side of the room. "We'll see about that!" Jab, jab.

Morgan, the younger of the two siblings, stretched his limbs languidly across the fine leather couch, watching the angry display being played out in the living room, a smirk residing on his lips.

"What has your knickers in a twist?" His leg, hanging over the arm of the couch, swung slowly back and forth.

Gitty broke her tirade for a moment. "I'm surprised yours aren't. How can you tolerate not having magic to use?"

"Because, dear sister, I don't *need* magic to get my way. I have my," he waved a hand up and down his body, "*obvious* attributes."

Gitty grimaced. "Please. Don't make me sick."

Pulling to an upright position, Morgan stretched his long legs in front of him, tucking his hands behind his head.

"You're just jealous."

"Hardly."

"Then what's your problem?"

"I don't fancy living my life in pubs among the scum of the valley sponging off the pity of strangers. My plans include owning all I see."

Morgan rose from the couch and faced his sister.

"Good luck with that. Even the Others are wise to your quest for power. I'm going out. See you later." He moseyed out of the living room and down the hall.

Gitty gritted her teeth. Morgan might be her brother, but he was useless when it came to thinking beyond his next good time.

She glared at the source of the fingers of light stretching over the meadow. The owner of the Lending Library was an Other the local fae had embraced with open arms. Even Uther, the one-time leader of the night elves and her uncle, had taken a personal interest in the older female.

"Must be losing his sanity."

She spotted a pinpoint of red light glowing in the far distance. As hard as she tried, she couldn't sense the origin of the light.

"I hate not having my magic!" She smacked the wall with her hand, immediately regretting the action. Bolts of pain shot up her arm.

"Damn it!"

Turning on her heel, she tramped out of the room.

## Chapter Two

Linda Brown, Librarian to most of the fae, peered down the entry lane, the cinnamon coffee exploding on her tongue. Spring was evident by the riot of color lining the road. Mist settled gently on the new foliage stretching to greet the sun. She sighed, a contented sound followed by a slow-forming smile. Her keen hearing picked up the subtle flutter of tiny wings.

Chrissy, the resident wood nymph, languidly made her way to the edge of the chair and, back-winging furiously, settled on the arm.

"Librarian?"

"Yes?"

"Would you like a refill?"

"Thank you, no. I'm doing fine. Your new coffee drink is heavenly. I think we need to create a name for it. What about *Cinnamon Chrissy*?"

There was a quick flapping commotion as the little nymph moved to face the librarian. Her deep violet eyes were wide with excitement.

"Really?"

"You did suggest and create it."

The nymph flew a loop-de-loop.

"Whohoo!" She buzzed around, settling once again on the arm of the chair, humming a tune the librarian recognized as an ancient Celtic song of celebration.

"Librarian?"

"Hhmm?"

"What are we going to do about May Day?"

"I'm not sure. What do you normally do?"

"We have a celebration of several days with dancing and feasting."

"I'll let you handle the planning. Just tell me what you need, and I'll do my best to provide it."

Silence stretched between the unusual friends.

"Chrissy?"

"Uh-huh?"

"You okay?"

"Uh-hum. Just trying to figure where to start."

Librarian smiled. The nymph had come such a long way from their first meeting when she'd tumbled into the library, disoriented and trembling in fear. The coffee shop and restaurant portion of the library ran smoothly under her guidance. A faint rustle of wings interrupted the librarian's thoughts.

"I think I'll start setting things in motion. If you need me, I'll be in the kitchen." The tiny figure zipped through the door, disappearing into the building.

Linda opted to stay on the porch and enjoy the sweet smell of the valley as the spring showers commenced to lightly sprinkle the earth. Through the mist, she spied a figure hiking up her driveway. Something familiar about the gait tickled her memory; the stride so confident, head held high.

*Night elf?*

Heat rushed to her cheeks, coloring the fair complexion. Stirring from her chair, she stood and stretched her legs. Her view of the traveler was better from a standing angle. There was no doubt as to the identity of the lanky man who assuredly strode to her front porch.

"Beautiful day, Librarian. Don't you think?"

"Yes, it is." Her cheeks glowed a healthy pink. "How've you been, Uther?"

"Well, I have a great hunger and thirst. Have you bread and drink available?"

"Let me speak with Chrissy. Please..." she indicated one of the chairs near a table, "...rest your feet. I'll be back soon."

Uther allowed a smile to cross his lips. This lovely woman whom the fae community had taken to their ranks so loyally made his heart pound. Removing his cape, he lowered his tired frame into the offered seat and leaned back to admire the scenery. His eyes threatened to close and would have had Linda not brought him a glass of water and several slices of fresh made bread. He could smell the delight before she placed the plate in front of him.

"Oh, my. It has been some time since I sank my teeth into the likes of fresh bread."

"You can thank Chrissy. I don't know why that little wood nymph is so determined to learn all the human tasks there are to living, but it's been a blessing in disguise. She really does make the best bread in the valley."

Uther slathered butter on the still warm slice and bit into the concoction. His moan of appreciation tickled Linda's heart. Sensations long forgotten started to make her uncomfortable.

"Would you like to try one of her coffee drinks? They're really quite good."

He held up a finger and slumped against the chair. "How anything can be as heavenly as this bread I don't know, but I'll try one of her coffees."

Linda noted the relaxing of his shoulders and settling of his body. *Good. Maybe, he'll stay longer than a day or two. Wait! Where did that come from?* She hurried to the kitchen, slowing as she neared the door. A gentle knock to alert the nymph to her presence was given.

"Yes, Librarian?"

"Could you make one of your Cinnamon Chrissy's for Uther?"

The little fae buzzed to face Linda. "Uther's here?" Her violet eyes danced with delight.

"Yes. He just arrived and is tired and hungry. I thought he could do with a tasty pick-me-up."

"Where's he staying?" Her wings shook with excitement.

"I…I hadn't asked him." Linda's brows knit together. "Why?"

"He used to stay with the Sauns when he came to visit. But he can't stay there now."

"Hhmm, you're right. I suspect the welcome mat wouldn't be set out for him."

"I'd offer my tree, but I don't think he'd fit." Chrissy tapped her finger on her chin, forehead crinkled in thought.

Linda burst into laughter.

"What?" Chrissy frowned.

Shaking her head, the librarian settled into a warm chuckle. "The picture of Uther trying to squeeze into your home just hit me as funny."

The little wood nymph tried hard to hold her serious look but was soon giggling.

"It would be funny, wouldn't it?"

Linda nodded. "What say we brew up some of your magical coffee for our night elf?"

Chrissy set to putting her talents to use, whipping up her cinnamon specialty. Linda carried the steaming mug to the front porch. Toeing open the screen, she headed toward the table Uther occupied.

Legs stretched in front of him, the night elf sat with his head against the building. His arms were folded and his platinum eyelashes rested on his tanned cheek. Linda stopped in her tracks and sucked in a deep breath.

*He's magnificent; so long and muscular.* She set the steaming coffee cup on the nearest table and retrieved his cape from the back of a nearby chair. Gently, she covered her sleeping visitor.

He stirred and blew out a deep sigh.

Linda froze. When Uther shifted and his breathing deepened, she backed away.

"What am I going to do? You can't sleep on the porch for the next couple days. There's a real possibility of the temperatures dipping." She muttered gazing at the form of the man whose looks made her heart pound. *Wait a minute!*

The cup of coffee trailed cinnamon scented steam into the library.

"Didn't he like my coffee?"

7

Linda recognized the hurt tone of the wood nymph. "He didn't even take a sip."

"What!"

"Hold on, Chrissy. I went out to give him the coffee and found him sleeping in his chair. Who knows how many days he's been traveling? I didn't see a vehicle or horse, so I can only assume he was walking. I'll bet he's just exhausted."

Chrissy winged to the window and peeked out at the slumbering night elf.

"Too true. Where's he going to stay?"

"When Donald, my husband, was alive we used to go camping in the Three Sisters Wilderness area. Somewhere in the shed out back I think I still have some down filled sleeping bags he brought home with him from his time in the service. I can air them out and provide some comfort from the elements for Uther. He'll be able to use the floor of the library after we close up at night."

Chrissy winged to face the librarian. "What if he says no?"

Linda shrugged her shoulders. "I don't know."

~ * ~

She wrapped her grey woolen sweater to her body and shivered. "Feels cool." The librarian hadn't been down the trail to the shed in several years. When her husband died, she couldn't face the memories stored in the eight by ten building. Placing her hand on the lock of the hasp, she pulled in a deep breath and turned the handle. Squealing unhappily, the warped door opened with difficulty.

Linda covered her nose to ward off the pungent smell of mildew. "Whew! I should've done this ages ago." She leaned in and grasped the thin string hanging from the socket of the bare bulb Donald had installed. The glare from the fifty-watt light momentarily blinded her. Recovering from the brightness of the light, Linda took a second look and groaned. Cobwebs blanketed everything in sight. She'd need to give the place a good cleaning before she'd be able to find anything.

Sighing in resignation, she turned out the light and closed the door. At the moment all she wanted to do was wash her hands in the stream and pull clean, crisp fresh air into her lungs. A hint of mildew clung inside her nostrils. Her throat tickled from the dust and everywhere she looked at her clothes she saw dirt. The path to the stream ran past the property line to the east of the shed. The proximity was too much for her to deny the pull and heeding her heart and not her head, she strolled through the woods admiring the spots of wild flowers exploding in spring color. Clear water tumbled wildly through the rocky riverbed. Linda stopped. By summer's end, this mad, rushing torrent would dwindle to a gentle, meandering brook.

She knelt down and dipped her hands in the closest pool. Chills exploded on her arms, and she fell against the mossy bank from the shock.

"Wow! I knew this was snow runoff, but I figured by the time it got here, the water would've warmed a bit." Linda furiously rubbed her hands together then stuck them under each arm for warmth. Rays of sunlight streamed through the forest canopy and speckled the riverbank, enticing her to lean back and close her eyes. A gentle breeze ruffled her hair. Muscles unaccustomed to relaxation betrayed her. For the first time in many years, Linda felt calm and at ease. Quieting her mind would prove more of a challenge; however, the roar of water exploding over rocks and rushing to the ocean soon gentled her overactive brain. As the rumble of water faded to background, Linda began to pick out the songs of robins and scoldings of bluejays nearby. Swishing grass tickled her arms and the new leaves on the overhead branches rustled. The scene was bucolic, but deep in the pit of her stomach, Linda felt a nagging. Something was off. She realized the birds had stopped singing. Opening her eyes, she looked around as she lay on her back. When she couldn't find the source of her uneasiness in the treetops, she propped on her elbow and reconnoitered the landscape around her.

The bank on the opposite side of the stream appeared barren of life. No swaying branches from the few bushes near the water. Linda's gaze moved south in the direction of town passing over a downed tree. She'd started to turn to her right when her brain registered what she'd just witnessed.

In front of the log, crouching low to the ground, sat an animal the size of a bobcat. This creature, however, was completely black with glowing yellow eyes. And worse yet, the animal had her in its sights. The eyes didn't blink. Linda looked away and turned back to find the creature crouching lower. She could swear the pupils had enlarged. The cat appeared ready to pounce.

Linda clamored up, turning to bolt back home as quickly as her legs would carry her. She ran square into a muscular chest. A piercing scream left her mouth as she fainted.

~ * ~

Uther swept the librarian into his arms before she could hit the ground. His heightened senses detected a presence across the stream. He narrowed his eyes and spied the black cat crouched on the bank. The malevolent eyes took him in, and Uther heard a low growl from the same general direction.

*You are the traitor of your own kind.*

The animal's thoughts jolted Uther. He kept a steady watch on the animal as it rose and slipped into the brush at the edge of the river.

"Ooohhhh." Linda was gaining consciousness. "Where am I?" She tried to focus on the nearest object. When she registered the fact she was in Uther's arms, her fair complexion disappeared beneath a rosy wave of color.

"Ple-please put me down. I can manage."

She wiggled in his grasp, causing him to let down one arm. Linda's feet dropped to the ground with a thump.

"What happened?" The worry in his eyes sent her to blushing anew.

"I went to the shed to find a cot and sleeping bag for you. I didn't realize just how long it had been since I'd been inside. When I emerged, I felt a desperate need to wash the dirt from my hands and, I guess, I sort of…"

Uther spared her the embarrassment she seemed to be experiencing. "With the cat?"

"Oh, I was enjoying the beautiful day and realized I could no longer hear any birds. When I looked around that…that huge animal was glaring at me. I thought it was going to attack me. I'd gotten up to head back to the house when I bumped into you and, well, you know the rest."

He chuckled, a warm soothing sound bubbling from deep in his chest.

"I can't say I blame you. That creature is the biggest house cat I've ever seen."

Linda furrowed her brow. "Are you sure that's a house cat?"

Uther nodded. "I can be fairly certain it's not a wild cat. I've never seen a black bobcat in my life; not that there couldn't be any, but I've not seen them. What say we go back to the house? I'm fine sleeping on the floor. I've spent the last six months or so sleeping in places not as warm or as comforting as the floor of your home."

Linda felt the warmth of a blush touching her cheeks. *I'm too old to be blushing like a schoolgirl.* She tromped up the path toward the Lending Library.

Uther stifled the urge to chuckle. *She looks so determined.* This Other had captured his interest when the clans of the valley had gathered and stripped the night elves, Gitty and her brother Morgan, of their magic. She'd not backed down against the formidable pair. Knowledge circulating in the fae community spoke that she willingly opened her doors to any who needed assistance, asking for naught in return.

He opened his mind and issued a warning. *I'm not sure what you're up to, Lancelot, but if you or your master, Gitty, bring harm to this Other, I will string you up and use you for target practice.*

The air before him wavered slightly and he knew his message had been received.

## Chapter Three

The lithe figure gave a flip of the tail and caught the current of rushing water to beyond the spot occupied by the large black creature. Finding her favorite lichen covered boulder, Trickle tucked behind the stone barrier and watched the action above her. The wicked, black cat was in the hunter mode and crouched to attack another victim. She ran a delicate webbed finger down the jagged white scar marring the beauty of her scales. The vitriolic beast had caught her off guard and nearly made her the object of a meal. Had it not been for-- *His voice! He's close by.*

She poked her head from behind the rock and noted he held the female in his arms. Trickle allowed a wrinkle to mar her porcelain forehead. *Is she dead? Did that monster feline claim another victim?* Movement in the man's arms answered her query. Trickle watched the woman stomp off toward the building where her cousin worked.

*Must be the one Chrissy calls The Librarian.*

He stood on the bank of the river and she jumped when the sound waves carried his issued warning to all who could comprehend.

*Lancelot. That is the name of my enemy.* Swishing her tail, she moved to the center of the manic flow of water and peered at the bank where the cat had stood. *He's gone--good.*

~ * ~

Uther caught the flash of tail and undulation of golden hair.

"Trickle, my friend? Is that you?"

The tiny creature wiggled her way to his side of the river and peered up at him.

He held his hands in front of him as he spoke. "I've no net and I promise on my honor as a reformed Night Elf of the house of Saun, I intend you no harm."

The brown speckled green eyes regarded him suspiciously.

"If I had meant harm, would I not have kept you after the attack?"

He tried his best to give her an earnest look of honesty. He could only hope it would work.

The water fae slipped a delicate hand on a rock near the bank and pulled up, flipping around to sit in the best position to afford her a quick escape.

"How are you, night elf?" The words from the mermaid flowed eloquently over Uther's ears.

He smiled. The first rule to speaking with a merperson was to be armed against the bewitching tone of their voice. He murmured lowly. "Block."

The mermaid giggled. "Ah, but you are wary."

"Indeed, my watery friend, and still dry on the bank. How is your side?"

Trickle gently moved her hair, exposing the wicked white scar she bore from her attack. "It hasn't disappeared." She traced the route of the mark.

"Why don't you magic it away?"

"It's a reminder to me each time I pass my hand over the hard line to be more alert in my daily life. If you hadn't come along at the right time…well, I won't allow myself to become anyone's lunch."

Uther nodded. "A very wise move. Be careful. Lancelot appears to be hunting these woods, and I know he hates losing a good catch."

"I shall, night elf. *You* be careful. If my cousin Chrissy is right, you are next on the list of targets." She flipped water with her tail and spattered him. A giggle escaped.

Brushing off the droplets from his breeches, he rose from the bank.

"I will, little one, I will. Until next time." Uther watched the selkie dive under the turbulent rapids and disappear. Turning from the river, he made his way back to the Library.

~ * ~

He was aware there were selkies in some of the local rivers but hadn't seen one. On a hunch after the clan meeting where his niece and nephew had been stripped of their magical powers, Uther had followed them out of the building. He'd sent Linda the Librarian off to get him a piece of cake to occupy her while he slipped out the back door. Using his enhanced vision, he tracked the pair as they crashed through the woods to their home. They still believed their magic was viable and arrogantly issued spells to clear the pathway to walk. On many an occasion that evening, Uther was forced to cover his mouth so he wouldn't burst into laughter as the two night elves stumbled over bushes and tree stumps which didn't magic away.

When he'd decided the pair was well on their way to their home, he turned around and headed back. His senses were overwhelmed by fear. Following the path of the terror, he came upon a scene he would not soon forget.

Clutched in the paw of the massive animal Gitty Saun kept as a house pet, was a limp figure. One side appeared to be covered in scales while the other showed bare flesh and flowing yellow hair. Uther acted on instinct and blasted the animal with a magic command.

"DROP HER!"

The cat pulled in the paw, bobbling its prize and growling as the creature fell to the ground. It started to reclaim the booty when Uther threw a lightning bolt above the animal's head. Yowling in anger and fleeing as fast as the padded feet could move, the cat vanished into the dark night.

Uther dashed to the river's edge and was amazed to find a miniature mermaid bleeding profusely from a slash the length of her body. He knelt and lightly placed a finger on the open wound while uttering a healing spell. He had to repeat the spell twice before the slash closed completely.

Her body fit neatly into the palm of his hand and he was careful not to jar her as he carried her to the river. Water slowly filled his palm as he lowered her into her element. His heart pounded as he prayed this unique creature wasn't dead. Her eyes fluttered and she opened her mouth to scream.

"Ssshhh!!! We don't want that monster to know you survived."

Affirmation from the mermaid was all he needed, and Uther released her completely, watching her swim slowly on the river's top then, with a flip of her tail, slipping beneath the water.

He'd not seen her since that time. Spying the little selkie was a pleasant surprise. However, viewing the black monster, Lancelot, was not.

Uther groaned. He just knew Gitty and her brother Morgan were up to something, and the rest of the valley would be caught in the backlash.

# Chapter Four

Large golden eyes observed from the foliage the interaction between the fair mermaid and the night elf.

*So she survived. Not for long. I'll have that tasty treat before the next moon.*

Employing all the lessons his mother had instilled in him, Lancelot moved through the underbrush with stealth. He needed to get home and communicate with his master, Gitty. Time was of the essence. It was imperative she be told Uther was in the valley again.

Breaking into a gallop, the sleek black cat sprinted through the forest. He stopped to reconnoiter the meadow when he reached the edge of the copse of trees. The air teased him with hints of mice nearby, but he couldn't stop to indulge his love of the hunt. The mice would be there in the early morning hours.

Tall grass whipped against his face as he raced up the hill. The sun cast golden shafts of light through the windows as he entered the house by means of his cat door. A quick stop at his water dish then he marched into the empty living area. The air hung in angry waves.

*I'll check her room.* He padded down the hall, skittering to avoid being kicked as Morgan burst from his room.

"Get out of the way, you wretched animal," he scowled at Lancelot.

Growling lowly, the black animal bared his fangs then continued on his mission. He flicked his ears when the door to outside slammed and slowed his pace as he neared his mistress' room. Cautiously, he surveyed the scene. Clothing was haphazardly strewn over the furniture, and the dressing table chair lay on its side. Lancelot eased his way into the space and hopped up on the overturned piece. He sniffed the air and twitched his ears forward and backward to catch the sounds of his lady, but his efforts were met with silence. Straining his neck and focusing his concentration, the wavering of air and clanging of steel crashed against his nerves. There could only be one place from where these sounds could emit.

He jumped off the chair and bolted to the basement gym. He must get to his mistress and make her aware of the enemy in the valley. The crashing of steel against steel muted his thundering paw steps.

"I HATE not having my magic!" Crash! The metallic clang echoed around the practice area. Grunting and thrusting with barely contained anger, Gitty attacked the dummy again. Crash!

Lancelot flattened his ears. The noise permeated his head and made his fur stand on end. Yowling, he tried to get her attention.

"I hate this." Crash! "I hate this." Crash! "I hate this!" Crash!

Sweat rolled down the sides of her face, and Gitty swiped at her forehead with the back of her free hand. Out of the corner of her eye, she spied Lancelot.

"What are you doing here?" Something about his presence rubbed her the wrong way. *What good are you if I can't use magic to talk with you?*

She ambled to the window and peered at the valley below. The sword clattered from her hand to the floor.

Lancelot cocked his head as she tried to choke back a sob. *Crying?*

"Yes. What's it to you?" Gitty barked.

*Just haven't seen it before.*

"Well it happens to everybody so--" She stopped and whipped around to face him.

"I can hear you."

*Yes.*

"Ho...how?"

*Humph. You lost your magic, not your telepathy.*

Gitty watched Lancelot roll his eyes. Then she started to chuckle. Soon she was laughing and dancing around the gym floor.

"Whohoo! This is just the beginning! I'll get my magic back yet."

She wrapped her arms around herself and began to hum.

*There's a reason I wanted to talk to you.*

Gitty looked at the black creature and smiled. "What?"

*Uther is back.*

The smile disappeared from her face. "Are you sure?"

Lancelot narrowed his eyes. *Of course. He threatened me.*

"He threatened you? Where is he? Why is he back?"

He shook his head. *I don't know why he is here, but he's staying with that Other in her lair. He threatened me when I was watching her by the river.*

"Really? Hmmm. This might work to our advantage. We'll let Morgan have his little play date tonight, but tomorrow, we need to come up with a plan to regain our rightful place in this valley--and get rid of Uther in the process."

She reached down and ran her hand over the fur on the back of Lancelot's body. "This turned out to be a *wonderful* day. Come on, big boy. Let's get you a treat."

~ * ~

Gitty stretched her legs to the mahogany coffee table. Lancelot had curled up at her side and napped by his mistress. Save for a haunting melody she quietly hummed, the room was silent. When the backdoor slammed, Gitty jumped and Lancelot raised his head and emitted a low growl.

Morgan stormed into the living room and started down the hall.

"Home a bit early, aren't you, little brother?" She glanced at the wall clock, noting the time was only a few hours later than his departure.

"Yeah, well, maybe I missed my loving family."

Gitty noted the acrid tone and sneer on his face.

"Pray tell what happened?"

"Don't feel like it."

"Fine, but don't come crying to me when Uther walks in to your favorite watering hole and sweeps the ladies off their feet." She stared at the retreating back and smiled when Uther's name stopped him in his tracks. She watched in fascination as he slowly turned her direction, noting the loss of color in his face.

"Uther?"

"Yes, dear brother, Uther. He's back in the valley and staying with the Other who's captured his eye." She watched the normally icy blue eyes of her brother darken to a cloudy grey.

Visibly shaking and gritting his teeth, Morgan measured his steps as he entered the living area. "He's the reason my nights have become so miserable."

The faint whisper of a smile touched Gitty's lips. "I thought you said you didn't need magic."

His brows knit together. "I say a lot of things. Doesn't always mean they're true."

She feigned surprise. "Really? Why, Morgan--I thought you to be a man of honesty and integrity."

"Save it. How can you know for sure Uther is back in the valley?"

"Lancelot told me."

He opened his mouth to answer then snapped it shut, rolling his eyes. "Sure. And the cow jumped over the moon. How can you talk with the monstrosity of a cat without your magic, sister?"

Lancelot raised his head to glare menacingly at the male night elf.

Morgan took a step backward.

Gitty inspected her nails. She allowed the ticking of the clock to fill the silence for five minutes before answering.

"I may have lost my magic but not my ability to use telepathy. And Lancelot saw Uther on the riverbank behind The Lending Library."

Morgan groped behind him to locate the chair. Once having found the leather seat, he dropped into the buttery cushions. "Uther...here in the valley again."

Gitty hid a smile. "Yes. A bitter fact we have to live with; however, dear brother, what would you sacrifice to have your magic back?"

Morgan snapped his head up and stared at his sister. "How?"

"That's the question to answer before the rising of the next sun. I think a pot of coffee with sugar and cream is in order. We need a foolproof way to implement this plan. And this time, *Uther* will pay with his life."

# Chapter Five

Chrissy tumbled wings over toes backwards, throwing out her arm to grab the microwave handle. Wildly swinging from the chrome grip, she caught a flash of grey barrel past her, leaving a faint whisper of pine in the wake. Librarian's sun streaked haired danced in the wind caused by her rush through the kitchen. The crash of the door against the frame set the little wood nymph's teeth on edge. She winged into place on the kitchen counter and listened to footsteps skitter across the hardwood floors of the library's main room. A slammed door followed by silence ended the abrupt interruption to the tiny nymph's afternoon routine.

The small fae spread her delicate wings and loped across the main room to the closed door on the opposite wall. She hovered in front of the portal and keened her hearing to pick up sounds behind the barrier. Odd sounds of shuffling assailed her ears. She raised a tiny fist to knock on the door when Uther burst into the room.

"Linda! Linda! Where are you? Are you alright?" He searched the aisles of the bookshelves and opened the front door to check the porch. Spotting Chrissy, he moved toward her.

The fae whipped around and crossed her arms over her chest pinning her most fearsome glare on him.

"What have you done to her?" She cocked her head to one side.

Uther shrugged his shoulders. "Nothing."

"Really, Chrissy. He's done nothing."

The nymph zipped around to stare directly into the steel gray eyes of her Other friend.

"Then why were you making such funny noises in your room?"

Violet eyes widened as the little fae cocked her head.

"It's, well, it's not Uther's fault. Just my own issues that have taken me off guard."

Chrissy shook her head. "What?"

Linda clutched a book in one hand. "Would you set the water to boiling? I feel the need for some tea."

"Sure. What kind, Librarian?"

"Chamomile. The calmness of the brew will help to set my mood. Uther? Would you care to join me on the porch? We need to talk."

He raised his brows at the fae and dipped his head in acquiescence to the librarian. "Of course, my Lady. After you."

He held the door open and followed Linda to the table and chairs on the porch.

When she bent to sit in the chair, an item fluttered from the book to the deck.

Uther leaned over and picked up a photograph. Pictured was a beautiful raven-haired maiden attired in a long satin wedding gown. A crown of tiny crème-colored roses perched atop a black mass of curls falling loosely about her face. Her delicate hand was slipped through the arm of a striking, fair-haired young man in Navy dress whites. Both young faces were glowing. His hand covered the small fingers resting in the crook of his arm. She smiled shyly at the camera. His eyes were tenderly locked on her face.

Uther handed the photo to Linda. "This is yours, I believe."

Linda snatched the photo. She felt heat crawling up her neck. "Darn it!"

He settled in the chair next to hers. "I'm sorry. Did I offend you?"

She pushed out a big breath. "No. It's why I wanted to speak with you." She turned to face him.

She held the memento in her hand and examined the two young people.

"This is a picture of me and my husband on our wedding day. Donald had received permission to come home before he was shipped overseas to Vietnam, and we put together a rush wedding and reception. We had three days for a honeymoon, which we spent in Bend at a ski resort then he left for the war. For eleven months, I lived on pins and needles dreading every phone call, watching the road for the car that would bring the officials to my door to tell me he'd been killed. When he walked through the door of our home in Eugene two months early, I fainted. He picked me up and carried me to the couch.

"Your actions this afternoon took me back to that day so long ago.

"I've been embarrassed about my reactions to you when we're near each other. I'm too old to be blushing like a schoolgirl, yet every time you speak to me, I explode in waves of redness. I'm an old woman, Uther, and I don't have time to waste playing silly games. That's for very young people."

He looked into her steely gray eyes. "You are a beautiful woman, Linda."

"Was."

"*Are.* The bloom of youth isn't all a true man searches for in a woman; kindness, intelligence and courage are just as important. I listen to the tales of the woods and the fae who dwell there. Your acts of kindness are spoken of throughout the valley and into the mountain ranges as well. You've protected many of the lost fae and guided others who aren't sure where to go. You open your home and food stocks for all who would ask. What more could a man in his right mind ask?"

Her cheeks exploded with color. "Damn it."

Uther leaned toward her and ran his fingers down the soft skin of her cheeks. "It is a beautiful sight to see a woman who is still humble and appreciative of a compliment.

"As far as the game playing, I have entered into many a contest but don't toy with affections. When I gaze at you with caring in my heart, it's because I wish you to know how I feel. I, too, am too old to engage in the foolish deeds the young seem to feel necessary for their courting rituals.

"And, yes, my Lady, I intend to court you. I have but a few decades more before my time to leave arrives. I intend to enjoy those years with a companion of my choosing."

Linda looked up to find teal eyes searching her face. She allowed herself to act without hesitation and placed her hand on his.

"I'd given up on the idea of finding a companion to spend my time with when you arrived for the counsel meeting, and I lost my heart. However, you left, and I was bereft; happiness was slipping through my fingers--again. Many a year has passed since my Donald lost his battle with cancer. Most Others believe you get one chance at a forever love. When you arrived, my heart told me once-in-a-lifetime was a fallacy. Sometimes, just sometimes, life pulls a fast one on you."

Linda ran a finger down Uther's hand, noting the musculature of his fingers.

"Courting is an old word and concept." She allowed a blush to color her cheeks. "But one I love. I like the idea of being wooed."

Uther raised a delicate white eyebrow. "Wooed? Whew! What a sexy word." The hint of a smile touched his lips. He gently lifted her hand to his mouth and placed a kiss on the back.

"I, too, have waited another lifetime to find a suitable companion. I was beginning to lose hope until the counsel meeting. Your reputation made you an interesting person. However, you are an Other and usually we don't get along. Your beauty intrigued me, but I believe what won me over was how you stood up to Gitty and Morgan. No one has laughed in Gitty's face and lived to tell the story. I knew then I had to get to know this Other who, first of all, believed and was able to see the wee folk and second, could stand her ground with a power hungry female Night Elf."

Linda had been staring at the floor as Uther spoke. He placed his fingers beneath her chin and lifted her eyes to meet his.

"So, yes, I plan to woo you and, if the gods favor me, make you my companion until the end of our lives." He leaned toward her.

"Librarian! Librarian!" Chrissy buzzed past Uther and hovered directly in front of Linda.

Pushing a wistful sigh from her lips, she replied. "What, Chrissy? What has you in such an uproar?"

"That wicked black cat is in the back yard prowling around."

Uther pushed up from the chair and bolted to the back yard. "He'd better not be."

Linda stood and stretched her legs. "Are you sure?"

Chrissy gave a delicate shrug of her tiny shoulders. "Well, the animal sure looked like that wicked creature." She caught the corner of her lip with her teeth as she brushed her light brown locks away from her face.

Uther returned with a smirk on his face. One hand was behind his back as he climbed the porch steps.

Linda gave a wary look his direction.

"This..." he brought his hand around to the front. In his palm snuggled a tiny black and white kitten, mewling noisily. "...is the wicked black cat."

Linda felt her heart melt. "Oh, my goodness. Somewhere a mother kitty is searching frantically for this little bundle." She held out a hand to Uther.

He placed the little cat in the center of Linda's hand and slipped his arm around her shoulders. "To the best of my ability, I searched her memories and discovered this little girl was born nearby, but her mother went out to hunt for dinner and never returned. This little thing wiggled her way to your backyard because, even in the world of animals, you're kindness is widely known." He ran his finger across the downy soft fur of the kitten.

Linda let a gentle smile light up her face. "Well, I guess I'll make sure she has a home. Did you get a name?"

Uther chuckled. "She says her mom calls her Piggy because she's always hungry. How do you propose to feed her?"

"You can't!" Exploded Chrissy.

"And why not?" Linda noted the crimson color of the nymph's face.

"That...thing will grow up and eat us."

"I don't think so."

"Fine. Then I'm leaving." Chrissy started to wing back to the kitchen.

Linda heard Uther mutter beneath his breath.

The little wood nymph stopped mid-air, her wings flapping furiously.

"UTHER! Let me go!"

"Not until you come back and apologize to Linda."

"I won't be eaten!"

He withdrew his arm from Linda's shoulder and walked to face the little fae. Crossing his arms, he set his face in a fierce scowl.

"Do you think the librarian or I would allow such a thing?"

Chrissy stopped trying to escape and slowed her wings to a hover. "And just what can you do to stop the animal from eating me?" She stuck her fist on a hip.

Linda stifled a giggle.

"Are you or are you not a wood nymph?" Uther slightly tilted his head as he asked the question.

Chrissy huffed. "Well, of course, I'm a wood nymph." She swept her hand up and down. "Duh! Tiny person with wings?"

"Yeah, I can see you and so can the librarian. Why can the librarian see you?"

The little nymph threw up her hands and rolled her eyes. "Because I'm not using magic to cloak myself."

Relaxing his expression, Uther stood back, allowing the statement to hang in the air, a slow easy smile replacing the scowl.

The thunderous frown Chrissy had mustered slipped away. "Oh, yeah. I can do magic."

"Um huh."

"So I can stay invisible as far as the creature is concerned."

"Yup."

"Oh. But…"

Uther reached out and placed his two fingers around the fae, breaking the spell. He carried her to Linda and stood with the fae facing the kitten. The tiny creature trembled in his grasp.

"This is an extremely young cat. Her memories are faint about her life lessons. You have the ability to perform magic and can be seen by the creature or not as you so choose. Imagine, if you will, training this creature to protect you."

Chrissy wiggled in his hand. "What? These are wild animals that hunt birds and small creatures to eat. I'm smaller than most birds. How could this beast be trained to protect me?"

Uther lowered her closer to the kitten. "Right now, this little one is desperate for love. She'll imprint on the person who gives her the most love. Pet her, go ahead."

The nymph cringed and opened her mouth to scream.

Uther shook his head. "You survived much worse in the woods. Try it. If the creature looks as if she'll try to eat you, I'll snatch you away and keep you safe."

Grudgingly, Chrissy reached out an arm and quickly slid her hand across the nearest section of fur. The tiny kitten began to purr.

"SEE! It's warning me to stop."

Linda smiled. "No. That's the sound they make when they are happy. It's called purring."

Chrissy glanced at the sleeping creature. She had to admit it was attractive, but so many years of fear couldn't be wiped away in five minutes.

"Okay. I'll give it a chance, but the first time it lunges at me, I'm setting its tail on fire."

Uther nodded. "Fair enough. Now I'll release you. Stay or go as you please." He opened his hand.

Chrissy shot him one last look of disgust and buzzed into the library.

"How are you going to keep it from eating her?"

Linda chuckled. "I believe after this one has had some nourishment, I'll sit down and let her know who's the boss around this establishment. We both know it isn't me. After a few weeks, I'm sure Chrissy will have

Piglet dancing to her tune."

"Piglet?"

"Yeah. I like the sound of it better than Piggy. Shall we take this new member of my household inside and make a nest for her?"

Uther dipped his head. "After you, my lady."

# Chapter Six

Morgan lolled his head to one side of the couch cushion. His eyes hurt from tracking Gitty's march back and forth across the living room floor.

"What is your problem, sister?" Yawning, he set his booted feet on the coffee table. "Unable to hatch a winning plan?"

"Some input on your part would be helpful." Gitty stood at the window and glared. The pair had been kicking ideas around most of the night and nothing had struck her as feasible.

Morgan dropped his head forward, his eyes glazed by lack of sleep. "Just kidnap the librarian. Tell Uther you'll kill her slowly unless he gets the clans together and gives back our magic. I'm tired and going to bed."

Dropping his legs to the floor from the coffee table, Morgan rose from the couch and trudged down the hallway to his room.

Gitty watched his retreating back and glowered. "Kidnap the librarian, indeed." She moved to the window to stare morosely at the valley below, Morgan's ridiculous suggestion ruminating in her mind. She hated to admit it, but the idea was beginning to have merit.

"Well, why not? The plan has viability. Two birds, one stone; Librarian is gone and Uther will be too once his lady love is out of the picture. But how?"

Gitty worried her bottom lip, lines forming above her brow as she turned over one plan of attack then another. Morgan's idea was a good one, but she was stumped on the execution. Lancelot wound his way around and through her legs.

*Why not kidnap her while she sits on the riverbank?*

"Riverbank, uh, what?"

*I said why don't you kidnap her when she goes to sit by the river?*

"That's a great idea if we can guarantee she'll be out there when we're ready to move ahead with our plan."

*She will be.*

"How can you be so sure?"

*When you were pouting because you didn't have your magic, I started watching the library from the opposite bank for a chance to get even with those miserable little faeries. Every day when the light has started to dim, she sits by the river for a while.*

"I don't pout."

*What would you call stomping around the house muttering to yourself and ignoring the rest of the world?*

Gitty graced the black animal with a cool stare.

"I was...thinking."

*Same difference. You were acting irrationally--even for you. It's time you regained your rightful place in this valley. Sitting and...thinking...won't move the situation to where it needs to be.*

"How can I guarantee the librarian will be there?"

*A daily walk appears to be in your future. We're able to keep contact within the length of a meadow, but no further. If you stay back a couple of your long steps in the brush by the river, I can let you know if she's there.*

"That's all well and good, but the moment she sees me she'll start screaming and our plan will be for naught."

*Then we need to recruit Morgan to be part of the action. If he appears on our side of the river, she'll be so concerned with him she'll lose track of what's behind her. You can subdue her and we'll bring her to the shelter in the woods.*

"Won't Uther be able to sense her?"

*Not if we place enough sensory camouflage around the shelter. We can send a note to Uther with subtle references to a warehouse in town. Maybe he'll believe it, maybe not, but it'll buy time.*

Gitty gazed in amazement at the black feline sitting at her feet wrapping his tail around her legs. "Where did you learn all this?" She could swear Lancelot was smiling.

*I listen and learn from the best.* He doffed his head to her then began to lick his front paw.

For the first time in many a week, Gitty smiled. "I do believe we have a plan of action that will work."

Standing up and gracefully stretching his legs, Lancelot moved to the warm spot in front of the heater vent. Circling three times, he finally lay on the floor and proceeded to go to sleep.

The she-night elf flipped off the lighting in the room and let her eyes roam over the landscape of the valley and surrounding mountains. She rolled her neck and dispelled the feeling of dread that had hung over her for the last few months.

"Retribution."

Gitty liked the way the word rolled off her tongue. She allowed a small smile to blossom and humming a Celtic war song, wandered down the hallway to her room. With any luck, tonight she would have the best night's sleep she'd had in longer than she cared to remember.

~ * ~

Morgan heard low humming and the soft swish of Gitty's house boots pass his door. The sound of silence followed a snick of the latch. An involuntary shudder passed through him. Whatever she and her wretched cat had cooked up would wreak havoc on the valley and further alienate him from the local inhabitants. Light from the scented candle on the nightstand next to his bed flickered across his chiseled features.

He leaned against the rosewood headboard and watched the changing shadows on the ceiling. There had been a time in the highlands back home when he and Gitty were inseparable. She'd been the only opponent to best him at the sword, and her skills at the Longbow were touted throughout the highlands by the bards. It wasn't until they came to this wretched country with its backward farmers and huntsmen did Gitty's temperament morph.

The bonnie lass from Scotland who could drink, fight and cuss with the best of the boys became a shadow of her former self. When the love of her life, Glade, was killed in a battle between the fae and night elves, Gitty shut down completely, turning into the miserable elven being who currently lived in the room next to his.

As her attitude declined into sarcasm and scorn, she quit seeking his company for sword practice preferring to set up her own obstacle course and workout haven in the basement.

It didn't take Morgan long to come to the realization the way of life they'd been taught to live was fading into the past. He frequented the local pubs and, with his striking looks, developed a reputation as a ladies' man. After a fight or two with the farm boys, his position was secured in the community. That is until Gitty felt the need to tear apart the old oaks in the meadows.

"There was the dandy with the heavy Irish accent I dueled who lost, but I'm sure that had nothing to do with my getting kicked out of the pubs." Morgan checked the clock on the nightstand and blew out a breath. "Morning will arrive too soon."

He blew out the candle and crawled beneath his covers. His stomach was lurching with the anticipation of what scheme Gitty had hatched.

# Chapter Seven

The clatter of metal against metal woke Uther from a lovely dream of a fair-haired maiden with cloud grey eyes who was lavishing a great deal of attention on him. He stretched his lanky form. Despite his statements about not needing anything but a blanket, Linda had scrounged a cot, his feet hung over the end, and several sheets and blankets to cover the canvas bed. Somewhere in the area behind her door, she'd located a pillow. The cover smelled of fresh spring days with a hint of warm spice. Sleep came easily within his warm cocoon between the aisles of the library.

The noise increased with the hour, and Uther gave up and crawled out of his bed. Rubbing his eyes, he pulled in a deep breath. The pungent smell of mountain coffee raked across his taste buds. He stumbled into the facilities and completed his morning routine.

Replacing the gentle warmth and sunshine of the previous day were light showers.

"Coffee?"

Uther had been staring out the front windows of the building and started when Chrissy spoke.

"Yes. I'd love a cup of black coffee."

She buzzed back to the kitchen and Uther heard the metallic clatter again. Curiosity got the better of him and he tiptoed to peek his head around the door. The little nymph was cooking by dancing in the air and on the tops of the pots and pans. The food on the stove was bubbling and hissing as she danced her magic to prepare breakfast.

"Oh!" She stopped when she spied Uther peeking in the doorway. Pointing at the cup on the counter, she muttered. "Warm."

He watched the steam rise from the mug. "Thank you." Grabbing the mug, he strolled through the aisles to the front door and went out on the porch. There was coolness to the air punctuated with moisture, sending a shiver down Uther's back.

"Damp." The coffee cup rested on the rail of the porch as his gaze was pulled to the road. Raindrops splattered on the asphalt creating a patchwork of lights and darks, rivulets of water racing to the sides.

"Yes, but good for the garden."

Uther jumped. "I didn't hear you walk up." He could feel the warmth of her smile.

"You were so intent on something down the road I really didn't want to scare you. Guess I did anyway, didn't I?"

The abashed expression on Uther's face let Linda know she had guessed correctly. "What has you so serious this morning?"

He took a sip of the cooled coffee. "I can't explain it very clearly, but I have a very bad feeling the Sauns are planning something. We both know nothing good comes from that."

Linda nodded her agreement. The last time the Sauns had planned something, they came close to eliminating all the oak trees in the area. Chrissy had fled from the demolition of her ancient home and stumbled into Linda's home library. It was a meeting of destiny as the two were closer than ever.

Uther faced Linda. "Please promise me you'll be careful."

She took a breath to protest.

"I know of what I speak. As much as it pains me to admit it, my thinking was very close to theirs until I met a few Others who changed my mind." He leaned in and brushed a soft kiss across her lips.

Linda felt her knees wobble and she closed her eyes. His touch set her ablaze. Her stomach flipped. Parts of her body she thought long dead were reacting in ways she'd forgotten. White spots appeared before her closed eyes, and she realized her need to breathe.

Heat swarmed up her neck and across her cheeks. She pulled away. "Oh, my."

Uther picked up her hand and with his thumb rubbed across the soft skin on the top. "You, my lady, are special, not only to me, but to many others through out this valley. Should any harm befall you, I'm not sure anyone could stop the fae from declaring all out war on the Other inhabitants of the meadow."

"Baloney. The Others of this valley are ignorant of the magical population who live here. They choose not to see what's right in front of them. They couldn't be blamed if anything happened to me because we both know the anger comes from the hill above us."

"You speak the truth, my lady. Please give me your word you'll take care with your daily routines and should you wish to venture away from the house, you'll allow me to accompany you."

Linda frowned. "I think you worry too much. I'll be fine but just to make you happy, I'll get hold of you if I feel the urge to take a stroll in the woods. Will that make you happy?"

Uther smiled. "Yes. I know asking you not to go outside are fruitless, so this will give me some peace."

Before either of the two could speak again, a tiny figure buzzed out to face them.

"Enough talk. Breakfast is served."

The night elf and Other stared at the wood nymph hovering between them. Crossed arms and a ferocious scowl convinced them argument was futile. Uther offered his arm and Linda slipped her hand through the crook of his elbow, strolling inside to the café.

On a table covered in an ivory tainted linen cloth, sat a sumptuous feast; eggs and bacon were accompanied by toast and pancakes. Fresh butter and warmed syrup were placed near the pancakes. Real porcelain plates and silverware resting on linen napkins that matched the cloth finished the picture. Gracing the center of the table was a crystal-cut vase holding a single daffodil.

"Wow." Uther pulled out the chair for the Librarian.

"You can say that again." Linda pulled the napkin from beneath the silverware and placed it opened on her lap. "You've outdone yourself,

Chrissy. This looks amazing and appetizing at the same time."

Linda observed the nymph's face color a deep pink.

"Thank you, Librarian. Now, no more talk--eat."

"Yes, ma'am." Uther winked at Linda as he reached for the eggs. "Don't have to ask me twice."

Linda watched him shovel several eggs onto his plate as he grabbed for the bacon. The hint of a smile dimpled her left cheek. *Haven't seen a man eat this well since before Donald got sick.*

"Don't tell me you're one of those Others who pretend not to eat until after the man has left." Uther snagged two slices of toast and with his knife slathered big globs of butter on each piece.

"Nope. Just didn't want to lose a finger or get my hand stabbed." She slid one egg and a couple pieces of bacon to her plate. Quickly snatching some toast she used her spoon to cover the top with homemade blackberry jam.

Silence filled the room as the food disappeared. When both plates were clean, Chrissy magicked her special coffee blend for them to top off their meal.

"I think you should tell Chrissy." Uther stretched his legs in front of him and took a sip of the cinnamon concoction.

"No. She worries enough without adding to it." Linda absently stirred the liquid.

"If you don't, I will. I want this land protected by as many entities as possible. I know how devious the Saun clan can be when they feel they've been wronged. Unfortunately, my lady, you stand in the center of their target right now."

"Fine. If you want to tell Chrissy, go ahead, but I won't put anything more on her."

Uther watched Linda gather their plates and stop at the kitchen door, knocking gently.

"Chrissy?"

"Yes, Librarian?"

"I need to get the dishes done and I believe Uther wants to speak

36

with you."

The little nymph peeked around Linda's shoulder to the table. "Why?"

"I think you should ask him."

"Okay." She fluttered casually toward the table stopping just in front of Uther. Turning, she glanced at the librarian.

Linda made a shooing motion with her hand. She watched the tiny fae straighten her back and hover in front of the night elf.

Faced with such a show of courage, Uther cleared his throat in an attempt to keep from chuckling. "I would like to ask a favor of you."

"Why would I grant you...anything, night elf?"

Uther tipped his head in agreement. "Point taken. However, what if the favor had to do with the librarian?"

"Well, that's different." Chrissy rolled her eyes.

"As I thought. I fear for the safety of the librarian. I have an unsettling feeling the Sauns will attempt to harm the librarian in some way."

A wrinkle marred the forehead of the wood nymph. "Why would they do that?"

"They are aware I have...feelings for her. As they no longer have magic because of something I did and the Librarian supported, what better way to get back at me than by harming her?"

Uther watched the wings of the nymph tremble.

"They wouldn't DARE!"

"Ahh, but they would, and I'm afraid they will. That's why I need your help."

"What can I do?"

Uther watched the worry on the little face turn to fierce determination.

"Put the word out. If any of the wee ones see the night elves from the house on the hill acting...odd, even for them, please let me know. I'll do what I can to make sure the librarian is safe. Any help your people can offer will be greatly appreciated."

"I'll leave the rest to you. I need to find a permanent place to stay." He unfolded his frame from the chair.

"If the librarian is in danger as you state, would it not be better for you to stay and guard her?"

Uther watched a tiny eyebrow raise in question. *Linda is right. This little wood nymph is very quickly adapting to human ways.* "You're right. I just wanted to spare her from the gossip of having a single man living in her home."

Chrissy humphed. "As if our people ever worried about the rumors and gossip of the Others."

Uther had to agree. The fae community worried very little about the moral boundaries set by the Others. He dipped his head in acknowledgement at Chrissy and went about the task of clearing up his sleeping area. The doors would soon be open to the Lending Library, and the place would come alive with the flurry of tiny wings. The fae in the community used the building as a safe haven to gather and update each other on the activities within the local population.

From the corner of his eye, he spotted Chrissy streaking out the back door. *Wouldn't want to get in her way.* He could only hope she was carrying out the task he'd asked of her. His instincts set his nerves on edge and he was certain Gitty and Morgan would be planning some retaliation in the near future.

The silence from their household defied the nature of the two spoiled night elves and it worried Uther. Anything concerning the Saun clan concerned him. As a former active member, he knew the mindset of the family. They didn't tolerate defeat well and he found himself disquieted at the thoughts lingering in his mind.

"I can only hope the fae will band together again to protect the librarian."

# Chapter Eight

Soft leather, moccasin-styled boots hugged the feet of Morgan muffling his footfalls down the hallway to the kitchen. His only thought this morning was of a rich hot cup of coffee. Aromatic whiffs of the potent bean drew him closer to the counter and his reward.

"Morgan!"

The tall night elf groaned. When his sister bellowed, he was usually in trouble. He set a mug from the cupboard on the counter and poured precious brown liquid inside.

"MORGAN!"

Throwing caution to the wind, he didn't answer but took a swig of the life giving fluid. Searing pain racked his throat, sending him into a coughing spasm.

"What?" he croaked.

Gitty's measured gait put him on guard. Her normal mode of travel was to barrel her way through, heedless of anything in her way. Most valley folk had learned to step back when they saw the statuesque blonde headed their direction.

"Good. We need to talk about the plan to get back our magic."

Blowing across the top of the cup, he lifted his eyes to stare at this sister. "What plan?"

"Again, I've had to come up with everything. So sit there and listen while I explain how we're going to accomplish our plan."

*Our plan?* He'd not submitted any input into the plan. How was it *our* plan? He could guarantee if anything went wrong he'd be the only one to pay.

Gitty filled a mug with coffee, adding sugar and milk to the dark brew. Beckoning her brother with a finger, she moved to the living room and sat on one end of the couch. Morgan followed her into the high-ceilinged room choosing to sit in the tufted leather chair near the fireplace.

"Your suggestion last night got me to thinking…"

"What suggestion?" Morgan furrowed his forehead.

"The suggestion about kidnapping the librarian."

"Wha? I, I, I didn't make any such suggestion."

Gitty watched the color drain from his face. She pushed an exasperated breath between her lips. *Constitution of a jellyfish.*

"Right before you skulked off to bed you said, 'Why don't we just kidnap her?' The more I thought about it the better I liked the idea."

"I was being sarcastic. I didn't really mean it." Morgan's hand shook as he lifted the mug to his lips.

"Of course you were being sarcastic. It's one of the things you do best. However, the idea took root. I think we have the means, without magic, to take back what's ours."

Morgan stared at his sister. She'd hatched some pretty wild ideas to get what she wanted before, but this was--insane! Without magic they risked being caught and taken to the Others jail…for life.

"Well, I think I can safely say you've lost your mind. I need more coffee." He pushed up from the chair and snatching his mug, disappeared into the kitchen.

Gitty ground her teeth but waited for him to return.

"What makes you think we can pull off taking the Librarian from under Uther's nose while all those miserable little fae people are meandering around her?" Morgan set his coffee on the side table and dropped into the chair.

Agitation drove her to stand. It took all her restraint not to start pacing.

"I have it on good authority the librarian goes to the river around the same time every day…and she goes alone; no fae, no Uther."

"Right. Who is this good authority?" A sneer began to form on

Morgan's face.

"Lancelot."

"Ha! Now I know you've been into the liquor cabinet. We don't have our magic, so how can you communicate with your...pet?"

*Because you both still have your telepathy.* The aforementioned animal padded in and started rubbing against Gitty's legs.

*I'm hungry.*

Morgan sat, blinking his eyes in disbelief. "It's a trick. You've learned to throw your voice." He pointed a shaking finger at his sister.

Gitty shook her head. "I can't believe we have the same parents. You're an idiot, you know? Mental telepathy isn't magic. That's why we can still talk with Lancelot. I'm going to feed him then we'll continue this discussion." She strode to the other room.

Morgan heard the banging of silverware against the cat's bowl and clatter as the spoon was dropped into the sink.

Gitty strolled into the lounge and dropped to the couch.

"I think you need to take up a hobby."

"Do you now? And what would that be?" He cocked his head to one side and proceeded to cross his arms.

"Fishing." A sly smile tilted Gitty's lips.

"Okay. That's it. I hate fish. I hate fishing. I won't put squishy wiggly worms on a hook and throw it in the water to stand around for hours doing nothing. I can't stand the thought of cleaning them, and if you don't eat them, what's the point of fishing?" Morgan scowled at her.

"You won't actually be fishing."

"What?"

"You'll be observing the librarian and waiting for a good time to let me know when to grab her." She watched a puzzled expression replace the scowl. "You need to start appearing on the opposite bank of the Lending Library for the next week to ten days. Once you become a fixture, she'll give it no thought whatsoever. Observe the time she comes out and when she leaves. Once we have her pattern established, we can choose the optimum time to grab her and slip away."

"Yeah, but won't she recognize me?"

"Not if you wear fishing gear and a big hat to cover your face."

"Just where are we going to put her? This is the first place they'd look."

"Eons ago, after the war in the valley, I took the time to provide myself an escape from the insanity of this house. My cabin is five miles due north from this location."

She watched the wrinkle in Morgan's forehead reappear as he contemplated this information.

"How do we get there? The area you're talking about has no roads."

"That's right. The only way in or out is on horseback."

"Right. So we drag this Other, on horseback, to some cabin in the woods until...what? She dies of starvation? Or are we going into the business of murdering people?" Morgan pushed up from the chair to refill his mug. He wandered back to the chair and took up his position.

Gitty shook her head and sighed. "Again, I have to wonder how we can have the same lineage. No, we won't starve or murder her. That would defeat our reason for kidnapping her. We'll put her across one of our saddles carrying her to the cabin, which by the way is continually stocked with a month's worth of food and water. One never knows when the need will arise to take some 'alone' time."

"Just how are you going to take her without a ruckus?" Morgan lifted a brow in question.

"If you'd stop interrupting me, I'd be able to lay out this plan and fill in all the details."

He held up a hand and settled back in the chair. "Please...educate me."

"We don't have enough time for that. I'll just fill in the blanks so you can stop whining like a little girl. Each day you go to the riverbank to fish, Lancelot will accompany you until you've seen the librarian come out and go back into her library. After a week or so..."

Morgan groaned.

Gitty shot him a withering glance and he refrained from making further noises.

"As I was saying…when you've established a routine of fishing on the bank, the librarian should relax. During the second week, you'll need to ride your steed down the hill. I'll be out for an afternoon ride waiting for Lancelot to tell me when the time is right. I've devised a way to knock her out without leaving any physical marks. Once I've accomplished that feat, I'll throw her across my saddle, and from there we'll head to the cabin avoiding any contact with the locals.

"At the cabin, we can restrain her. I've located one of the old cameras that spit out pictures to use in making our demand. One shot of her tied up and gagged and we'll have Uther eating out of our hands. By my calculations, we should have our magic back by the end of the month."

Silence followed the detailed explanation. Gitty watched her brother mull over the plan.

"What's the issue? I've contemplated all the possibilities and worked out things so neither of us will get caught. What's taking you so long to agree?"

"Do I have to wear those stupid looking waders?"

"What?" Gitty jumped up from the couch to face her brother. "You're worried about how you'll look!" She stomped to the kitchen and slammed her cup on the counter.

"Complete idiot. The fates are against me. First, a total brainless wonder like Morgan as a blood brother then our father goes and marries a gnome. A gnome! And I'm saddled with that miniature female wanta-be-warrior, Tiamoon. What a joke. I should just liquidate the assets we have here and move back to Emerald Isles." Scrubbing the cup, she muttered between clinched teeth.

"Uh, Gitty?"

"What?" She turned to glower at her brother.

"I think your idea is really great. When do we start?"

She stared at him; a nervous smile attempted to blossom on his face. He shuffled from foot to foot and kept pushing his long hair behind his shoulder.

"Truth be told…I've been miserable without my magic. It seems I've overestimated my attraction to the Other women. Once they discover I have no income, they melt away. I'd love to have my magic back."

Gitty realized his reason was shallow, but whatever it took to have him work with her was fine. "We'll start tomorrow." She watched his shoulders drop as he relaxed.

"What time?"

"Lancelot says she takes a break around three in the afternoon. You'll need to be on the bank a little before. When you get there, pretend to be setting your line then monitor her actions. You might want to nod her direction so she isn't alarmed by your presence. Check the time she goes in then stay for thirty more minutes and pack up and leave.

"We'll continue this for the week, and about Wednesday of the following week, we'll make our move."

Morgan nodded and drifted off toward his room.

Gitty watched his lackadaisical shuffle and mentally kicked herself. *If we pull this off, I'm leaving this offensive valley and all the inhabitants behind.*

# Chapter Nine

Chrissy zipped through the door Linda had specially made for her. She flew as fast as her wings would allow and arrived at the riverbank breathless. Slowing her speed, she surveyed the river, trying to recall the outcropping her cousin Trickle had described to her. About to give up, she caught the flash of flowing golden hair. She winged to the top of the water then hovered.

*Trickle.* The gold flash moved nearer her position. *Trickle, it's Chrissy.*

Rising from the water, the golden hair undulated down her back as the mermaid immerged from the depths of the river.

*Cousin. What can I do for you?*

Long ago the cousins had agreed to communicate nonverbally to keep eavesdroppers at a minimum.

*Uther has asked me to convey to you the urgency of keeping an eye on the river.*

The mermaid swished her tail and her eyes lulled seductively.

*You mean the handsome, gentle night elf?*

Chrissy huffed an impatient breath. *Yes, the same one. Could you keep you mind off your tail? Anyway, he's afraid his niece and nephew might try to harm the librarian.* She watched Trickle's eyes light up.

*Nephew? Is he as handsome as Uther?*

*Come on, Trickle. Yes he's as handsome as Uther, but don't you…* Chrissy stopped and stared at the flow of golden curls waving in the current of the stream.

*That might just be the answer.*

*What?* Trickle rolled a backward somersault coming up in the same place.

*If you happen to see the very tall, very handsome Morgan, feel free to charm him the best you can. You might not be successful as he was once of the fae community but...who knows?*

Trickle cocked her head and narrowed her eyes. *What do you mean was once of the fae community? Isn't he any longer?*

A smile touched the lips of Chrissy, exposing a small dimple in her right cheek. *He and his sister sought Thomas' gold and were willing to kill all the Ancient Ones in the forest to find the treasure.*

Trickle chuckled. *Everyone knows Thomas is a braggart and liar. Why would they believe him?*

*He told them the treasure was around The Lending Library. When they arrived to dig up the fortune, the clan Chieftains were meeting, having banded together to find the culprit in the killing of the Ancients. So many fae had lost homes and been forced to move to Faetown, the elders were willing to put their differences aside until the mystery was solved.*

*Gitty and Morgan threatened to use their magic and, consequently, it was taken from them. They are as vulnerable as the Others.*

Trickle fluttered her tail and giggled. *Ooo, a mortal for my very own. I've wanted to come out of the river, but only for a good reason. This might be fun. Maybe I'll just keep him.*

Chrissy started an ascent. *Have fun. Let me know if you see him.*

The little mermaid zipped around the river singing, *A man of my own, for my hearth and my home.*

Chrissy couldn't stop the blossoming smile. The night elves were in for a big surprise if they thought they could outwit the fae. *A big surprise.* She loped along the path to the Lending Library stopping every so often to admire the new growth of spring. This year the rain had fallen, just enough, to ensure spring and May Day would provide an explosion of color for the festivities. She spun around, lope-de-loping, before entering her door.

Time was quickly slipping away and she had so many things to do. With Trickle on the alert for the night elves from the back of the property, she needed to get the word out to the community to keep a watch on the nefarious two from the hill.

~ * ~

Uther had watched the lithe wood nymph zip from their conversation out the back door. A chuckle bubbled up from deep inside his chest and he marveled at the determination on the little one's face.

"I'd sure hate to be on the wrong side of that little fae." He stretched his arms above his head before standing and reaching for the ceiling. "Need to get some fresh air." Stepping out the front door, Uther meandered to the porch railing and surveyed the scenery. There was light chatter from the surrounding birds as new hatchlings tried their shaky wings in flight. A gentle breeze ruffled his long locks, and he pulled in a deep breath of the rain freshened air. The clouds last night had wept on the landscape but dissipated this morning, leaving a light layer of moisture over the budding earth. Everything felt...new. Uther smiled and straightened up. As he was about to turn and return inside, a movement on the driveway caught his attention. He stood watching in fascination as the black spot moved closer, revealing a small donkey cart pulled by some sort of wire-haired dog. In the driver seat, he recognized the being as a gnome.

Bram held the reins in his hand and let Silas take the lead. The two had been partners for all of Silas' life and could predict what the other was thinking a majority of the time. Silas, a terrier mix, was panting heavily as he slowed and positioned the cart in front of the Lending Library.

"Bram, my friend." He panted and folded his legs beneath him.

"Ahhh! Silas! Let me know before you do that." Bram grasped the front rail of the cart. "You nearly threw me over you."

"Sorry. I think you might want to, uh, cut back a bit on the mead. I do believe you have increased your girth." The terrier stood, leveling the cart.

"I think you, my friend, are too tired due to the Mrs.' condition. However, I'll take your advice into consideration. We have business to conduct. We can discuss this after we have spoken with Chrissy."

The terrier waited for his passenger to disembark before lying on the ground. "I don't recall getting a message. When did you hear from her?"

"I received a message from the Sky Network. The bluebirds were busy gossiping as I cleaned the cart this morning. Sorry I didn't let you know." Bram realized Silas was fast asleep. He shrugged his shoulders and shuffled to the steps.

"Morning."

Bram snapped his head up and lost his balance, tumbling backward off the steps.

Uther scurried down the steps toward the gnome.

"Don't touch me! You've already scared the life out of me. Don't make it any worse." Bram scowled dangerously, lifting his gaze up to stare into cool, blue eyes sporting a twinkle set in a tanned complexion. Long silver hair fell forward around high cheekbones and an amused smile touched the stranger's face. Yet, Bram knew this face was...familiar.

"Uther?" The angry frown disappeared as the stranger extended a hand. "When did you get back?" Bram allowed himself to be assisted off the ground.

"I returned within the last few days. I've been feeling anxious about the librarian's safety. How have you been?"

Bram dusted the dirt from his breeches as he climbed the steps to the porch. "I've been just fine. Work has been a bit slow in coming, but it's the time of year when most everyone is hunkering down in their homes. And you, friend? How is life treating you?"

"Mostly I've been traveling the back roads, keeping tabs on the fae community."

"While I would love to sit and chat, I need to speak to Chrissy. Will you excuse me?"

Uther extended a hand. "Of course."

Bram reached up and shook the night elf's hand and dipped his head moving through the Lending Library's entrance. He stopped to get his bearings within the building and allow his eyes to adjust to the darker room.

Humming directed him toward the kitchen.

Poking his head around the doorframe, Bram ventured a foot over the sill.

"Uhm, Chrissy?"

"AHHH!"

The clatter of dishes and silverware reverberated throughout the library.

"What the...Bram!" The flustered wood nymph fisted hands on hips and glared at the cart driver. "Watch where you're going! Look at the mess you made."

The gruff gnome furrowed his brows, the bushy slash marks of hair forming a dark sinister line above his eyes. "You're the one who called me. What do you need that is so important you'd use the Sky Network?"

Chrissy waved a delicate hand over the broken bits of dinnerware scattered upon the floor. Rising from their location, each piece found its corresponding mate and cleaved together, hovering above then lowering to the countertop.

Bram had to admit he admired the nymph's magic. Her temper, on the other hand...

"You saw Uther?"

"Aye."

"Did he fill you in on the reason for his visit?"

"I believe he mentioned something about the librarian."

"Good heavens, Bram, don't you ever get excited?" The little fae rustled her wings in agitation.

"What's the point? It's useless energy. What is it Silas and I can do for you, Chrissy?"

Pulling in a deep breath, the fae slowed the flutter of her wings to a hover before the gnome. "Uther believes the night elves, Gitty and Morgan Saun, will try to harm the librarian. He asked me to get the word out for the community to keep a watchful eye on them. If you see or hear anything that seems out of place for them, use the Sky Network to warn us as quickly as possible."

Bram lightly ran his fingers down his beard, trying to herd the coarse hairs into place. "I can make sure the word is spread. How will I be paid? I have a family and Silas' Mrs. just announced they're expecting-- again."

"You're joking, right?"

"No ma'am. My services cost. You can try the Sky Network and see how well that works, but Silas and I are dependable."

Chrissy felt the urge to throttle the meadow fae with her bare hands but kept her irritation under control. "You, Silas and your families will be the guests of honor at the May Day celebration; all your food and drink will be furnished for you by the community. Fair enough?"

Bram rolled the idea around in his head. "Sounds good. I'll be shoving off. We've got lots of work to do and not much time. Miss Chrissy." He saluted the wood nymph and spun on the ball of his foot, marching through the rows of books to the porch.

Chrissy magicked the silverware to the sink where she worked with the water and dish soap to again wash the utensils clean. Gone was the contented humming replaced by muttering and banging of the forks and spoons. Once she'd cleaned everything, she ordered the items to put themselves away. She needed to take a break and rest her magic. Slipping from the kitchen, Chrissy winged her way to the windowsill and settled in the high heel shaped recliner the Librarian had given her. The sun streamed through the boughs of the tall pines warming the spot where her chair sat. Chrissy considered contacting the Mouse Network to ask the animals to keep watch for any unusual behavior on the part of the night elves. She'd be certain to set the plan in action…tomorrow. Before too long, the sound of gentle snoring filled the corner of the room.

~ * ~

Bram nudged Silas from his nap with the tip of his soft boots. "We have work to do."

The dog yawned and stretched his front legs. "Going far?"

"Yup. All around the valley."

"Big payday?"

"Not quite."

Silas had stood and was stretching his back legs. He stopped and turned to Bram. "We're not doing this for free, are we?"

"Nope. We'll be the guests of honor at the May Day celebration. Everything will be provided for all our families."

Silas used his back leg to scratch behind his left ear. Spring always made his skin dry and itchy. "Guess that'll do. We ready to go?"

Bram climbed into the cart and grabbed the reins. "Let's head out."

"Where to first?"

"We'll start going west then circle the valley. Should be back home in a couple days."

Silas tugged against the weight of the cart and Bram, getting his footing and setting a walking pace he could maintain for the long haul.

Bram saluted Uther and turned his attention to the road. He pulled out a pipe and lit the bowl with a quick flash of fire from his fingertip. *Chrissy isn't the only one who has magic.* He settled in his seat and pulled in the sweet taste of his black cherry tobacco. This job was going to test the flint of both he and his friend Silas. *We can do it.*

"Silas."

"Yes?"

"Stop when we come to the fae community of the lower meadows. I need to speak with the clan chieftain. It's important."

"You got it." Silas knew this was Bram's way of saying he was going to nap.

The easy pace set by Silas eased the tension Bram had felt at the Lending Library. He puffed on his pipe. Silas' nails click-clicked on the road, lulling Bram's eyelids toward his cheeks. He slid the pipe from between his teeth and knocked the smoldering tobacco into a tin can he carried for just this purpose. Once he secured the pipe inside his vest, he gave in to the urge to snooze. He could rely on Silas to wake him when they arrived at the fae community.

~ * ~

Uther watched with amusement as the odd pair disappeared down the driveway. He wasn't sure what had transpired, but glancing in the window he noted the little wood nymph lay out in what looked to be a reclining chair. Her tiny wings were tucked beneath her form. Eyes closed, her face glowed with serenity. She was indeed a beautiful creature.

Venturing into the library, Uther scanned the area, his stomach clenching when he couldn't locate Linda. His stride quickened as he moved from one aisle to another. Using his last resort, he knocked on the door he knew led to her private area. The response was a hollow unanswered sound. *Where is she?* A clock tolled from within her room alerting him to the time. Eleven times he heard the bells chime. *Where is she?* The slamming of a door sent him charging into the kitchen area, knocking Linda askew. He reached out and grabbed her arms as she started to fall backward.

"I--I'm so sorry."

She narrowed a look his direction. "What is *wrong* with you?"

"I said I was sorry. Worry clouded my thoughts when I couldn't find you."

"Why?" Linda put the overflowing basket on the counter, removing dirt-encrusted carrots from the top of the pile. She ran water from the faucet over the orange roots and used her hand to loosen the mud.

"I'm really serious about you being careful. I have a bad feeling you're in danger."

Linda continued to wash the fresh vegetables. "I've lived this long in my home with no problems, and I'll continue to live as I please. I'm not stopping my life because you have a *gut* feeling I *might* be in danger. Since Gitty and Morgan no longer have their magic, what can they do?"

Uther ground his teeth. "My lady, I hate to be a pain, but I know this family, and I know how devious they are when they feel threatened. Your involvement in taking away their magic is paramount in their thinking of you as an enemy. *Please* be more careful."

C. L. Kraemer

Placing the carrots in the sink, Linda turned to face Uther.

He noted her stormy eyes take on a softness, reflecting a light dove gray color.

"I've been on my own for so long, I've become quite adept at taking care of myself. It's...difficult for me to realize someone else might care if something happens to me." Linda stepped toward Uther and rose up on her tiptoes to place a kiss on his tanned cheek. She watched him slowly turn a ruddy pink and lower his eyes.

"Well, someone does care. Will you take care--for me?" He raised his gaze to her amazed expression.

The sincerity and--angst--held within made Linda's breath catch in her throat. "I--I'll try to remember." A tremulous smile touched her lips.

"That's all I can ask." He straightened and glanced at the basket of vegetables. "Need help?"

Linda glanced at the cornucopia of greens. "Nope. This is women's work. Now, scoot out of my kitchen." Giggling, she'd grabbed a dishtowel and snapped at him with it.

"Don't have to ask me twice." Uther hustled from the room and made his way to the porch.

His gaze fell on the back of the cart disappearing down the driveway. Birds merrily called to each other across the greening meadow and the sun peaked through the tiny sprouts of new growth on the pine trees lining the lane. Serenity appeared to be the weather of the day.

Uther felt a shudder travel his body. It was quiet--too quiet. Everything in him screamed of trouble brewing, and the cause had two names, Gitty and Morgan Saun.

# Chapter Ten

Trickle lay on her back, slowly swishing her tail and watching the birds above the water arguing over placement of a nest.

"Silly beasts." She turned and swam to her cove. Wedged behind two rocks was a mirror she'd found on the side of the river. She gazed at her reflection, noting she was getting a bit thin and pale.

"Need to go top side for a day or two." The thought brought a smile to her face. She wiggled to the mirror and feeling along the backside, pulled an oblong piece of paper encased in plastic and a drying spell from behind the reflective glass. The paper had a picture in one corner and Trickle was amazed at how much it resembled her. She'd asked Chrissy to have the librarian tell her what it said, but her cousin had clucked her tongue in disgust, reading the black lines to Trickle. This piece of special paper was; what had Chrissy called it? Oh yeah, a driving license, whatever that was.

Trickle found the paper at the edge of the water and, on an impulse, dragged it back to her secret cove. She knew at some point it might come in handy. She was right. The last time she'd opted to go *above,* the paper had helped her to go where she wanted. She thought maybe there was magic in the paper because all the doors opened for her.

When she'd returned from her land adventure, she'd bargained a bit of simple magic for a small valise to store her human clothing. One of the few oak trees not bulldozed by the she night elf's company served as a storage and changing place, Trickle deposited the case deep in the hollow of the tree. She hoped it was still there. She'd have to ask Chrissy to help her come up with something to wear otherwise, and right now she wasn't willing to include her cousin in her plans.

~ * ~

"Really? I mean, really?" Morgan looked at the dark green, rubber wading boots, fishing hat and pole displayed on the couch. "You really expect me to wear these…hideous things? Not on your life. There's got to be another way."

Gitty was trying to keep from chuckling and not doing a good job of stopping herself. She burst into laughter.

"Oh my god, you should see your face. Ahh ha ha…" Rolling on the couch, clutching her abdomen, the she night elf was caught up in waves of hilarity. "I have to get a picture of this."

Morgan pulled up and straightened his back. "Then do it yourself." He turned and stomped to his room.

Gitty lay on the couch sniggering and trying to catch her breath. She'd better apologize to the drama king or they'd be back to square one and still have no magic. Sighing with exasperation, she moved from the couch and headed down the hallway to soothe her brother's ruffled ego.

She knocked on his bedroom door. "Come on, Morgan. Don't be such a baby. It's only for a week or two, no more. Just think…when you're done and we have the librarian, you'll get your magic back and everything will be the way it's supposed to be."

The door creaked open an inch. "I'm not wearing those hideous-- whatevers."

Gitty backed away. "Fine. But take them, anyway. They'll be good props. Anyone passing by will think you're actually fishing."

He ventured out of his room, keeping a wary eye on his sister. "If this works and we get our magic back, I want a proper apology."

She turned on her heel and strode to the living room. "I'll write it in the sky with my broom."

*Fitting.* Once in the living area, Morgan stood in front of the picture window, ignoring the view of the valley below. He turned his back to the glorious sunshine and faced his sister on the couch.

"When is all of this to happen?"

"I'd like to ride to the area today and give it a look-over to see how much camouflage you'll need. Lancelot will lead the way. Once we've seen the stream and the foliage on the banks, we'll have a better idea exactly where you need to stand to get the best observation point. That alright with you?" Gitty cocked her head and hitched her right eyebrow.

"Fine. I'll change and get my horse ready. I'll be in the stables when you're ready to leave." Morgan marched out of the living room and back down the hallway.

Gitty blew a breath between her lips. "My brother, the drama king." Shaking her head, she got up from the couch and ambled to her room to change to her riding leathers. The weather was a bit cool so she grabbed her insulated jacket and quilted leather gauntlets. Her horse could do with a good brushing.

She was at the back door when Lancelot appeared. "Where've you been?"

*Napping. It's what I do. Where are we going?*

Gitty opened the door, letting the cat out first. "I thought we'd ride to the stream behind the Lending Library and you could direct us to the best spot to keep an eye on the Librarian. I'm going to brush my horse first, if you care to join me."

*No thanks. I'll lay here in the sun until you're ready to leave.*

"Suit yourself. I'll call you." She turned to the black creature only to find him sunning himself on the step of the back porch, his eyes tightly shut.

The brisk walk to the stables energized the night elf and she entered the barn with vigor. Her most recent acquisition was a mahogany brown stallion bursting with spirit. His haughty manner and rippling flanks caught her attention the moment she saw him running through the fields of a local farmer in the valley. Buying the animal involved a great deal of bartering on her part, and she knew the man overpriced the animal to discourage her. What he didn't know was once Gitty decided she wanted something, nothing could dissuade her from that goal.

Glade whinnied the moment he caught wind of her scent.

"Hello, my beauty. How are you today?"

The stallion threw back his head and pawed the ground in his stall.

"Ah, good to see you're anxious to get out and run. We're going on an adventure, but first I'll give you a good brushing so you sparkle in the sunlight. What do you think?"

The animal, seventeen hands at the shoulder, lowered his head, allowing Gitty to scratch behind his ears.

She stood on her tiptoes and whispered. "I miss you so much, Glade. If I had to do it over again, I'd let you catch me this time." Gently rubbing the horse's nose, she gazed into the dark brown eyes. "I know you're in there. I can feel it."

Brown eyes blinked at the night elf and the steed pushed his nose against her hand. Gitty grabbed the brush from the shelf. She put Glade on a lead and freed him from the stall, tying the lead to a center post. With determined slow strokes, she brushed him from the tip of his nose to the end of his tail. She felt the ripple of his muscled body and sensed the excitement building within him. It had been too long since the two rode from the grounds. They were about to resolve that problem.

Clip clopping of horse hoofs broke Gitty's rumination as Morgan and his horse headed toward the exit of the stables. She gave one last swipe to the mane of her steed and preceded to place the hand-tooled, black leather saddle on his back. Completing the task of readying her ride, she swung up and trotted out the stable door as she donned her riding gloves.

"Get that, would you, Morgan?"

He glared at her as he moved to close the entrance. "I'm not your personal servant, sister. If you want my help on the project, you'd best stop treating me as though I am."

"Fine." Gitty removed a glove from her right hand and, placing two fingers to her lips, whistled for Lancelot. She pulled Glade to a stop to replace her glove and wait for the third member of their troop to arrive.

Strolling up to the mounted elves, the black cat stretched his legs in front of him and yawned.

"You ready?" Gitty touched her heels to the stallion's flanks.

*Yes.*

Morgan snapped his head around to stare at the cat. "I can hear him!"

"Bravo. Now let's get going. I want to find this place and get this reconnaissance over. I have other things to do with my time before we set this in motion."

The odd party of large black cat and two night elves on horseback cantered out of the stable yard and down the hill toward the valley.

# Chapter Eleven

Linda slipped out the back door and followed the trail from her garden to the bank of the stream. The sun was blessing her favorite spot, and she needed time alone to let her mind wander. Uther's intentions were pure, but he was being a bit of a pain about implementing them. After all, she was well over twenty-five and caring for herself was a daily ritual. She could spot danger the moment it appeared. As she sat and argued with herself, she succumbed to the warmth and peace of the moment. Linda laid back and closed her eyes--for *just* a moment.

~ * ~

Gitty let her body roll with the rhythm of Glade's easy gallop. The spring was in a teasing mood, providing sunshine and warmth to bath the valley. She allowed a moment of contentment to color her outlook--for a brief time. Her cat, Lancelot, sprinted through the tall grasses of the valley looking over his shoulder every so often to make sure she was still following.

His frantic gait slowed to a walk where upon he undulated behind a large bush.

"Lancelot." Gitty pushed an angry whisper between her teeth. "Where are you?"

*Come on. Use your mind. I'm right behind the bush staring at the librarian across the stream. That is what we came for, right?*

Gitty reined back on Glade's bit and dismounted in one smooth movement. Morgan brought up the rear, reining his horse to a walk before flipping his leg over the saddle horn and dropping to the ground.

"Shhh!" Gitty shot a nasty look Morgan's direction.

Straightening up, he tied his horse to a nearby bush. Morgan measured his gait as he inched toward the stream's edge. Rounding the mulberry, he spotted the form of the female the fae called Librarian. Bile rose in his throat. This being is the one who doomed him to a life of banality. Heat rose up his core and Morgan's vision blurred red around the edges. He took a determined step toward the stream.

Gitty watched her brother's slack features harden. His eyes locked on the human opposite their location. She'd never seen him so focused. When the color of his neck started to turn a deep pink, she knew Morgan had crossed the line of logical thinking. He was running on emotion alone and the consequences would be disastrous. She shot out a hand, grabbing the back of his duster to restrain him.

"WHA…!"

Tugging with all her strength, Gitty yanked him behind the bush and clapped a hand over his mouth.

"Ouch!" She snatched her hand to her chest. "Why did you bite me?"

His blue eyes were glacial. "You put your hand over my mouth. Why?"

"You were headed to the stream with blood in your eye. That's not the way I want this to go."

"I, what?" The surprise on his face was genuine.

"Little brother, I think it's time to go. I'll explain it as we head home."

Morgan leaned his head to look around the mulberry bush. The prone figure hadn't moved from the sunny spot. As he started to pull back, the glitter of gold flashed in his eyes.

Lancelot rushed the stream. *Mine, all mine!*

*Lancelot! You can fish later. It's time to go home and finalize our plans.* Gitty ground her teeth. If it wasn't her brother testing her limits, it was the single-minded cat.

Grumbling with each step, the black feline stomped his feet as he moved away from the stream. *I'll have that half fish yet.*

"Half fish?" Morgan untethered his horse and swung into the saddle. "What is the other half?"

*It resembles one of those dreadful faeries.*

"Really?"

Gitty turned and sneered to the lagging parties. "Get a move on. We don't want to be discovered because the two of you decided to have a leisurely conversation about fish. Move it!"

*Hmm, half fish and half fae.* Morgan's face brightened. *A mermaid.* He urged his horse on and was soon rolling the thought of mermaids around in his mind as he galloped toward the stables of home.

~ * ~

Trickle's scales itched. Something wasn't right, and she could sense an ominous force nearby. Swimming against the current near the rock-strewn bottom of the stream, she located a niche in the rocks by Librarian's favorite spot. Chrissy had entrusted her with the duty of keeping an eye on the human, and while she'd rather play in the currents, she had made a fae oath and was bound by the laws of the fae community to keep her word. She wiggled down behind a rock and clutched the lichen growing on the sheltered side. The nasty black animal skulked about the shoreline, concentrating on the area where Librarian usually sat. She crouched down. That's when *he* appeared.

His hair shimmered in the sunlight and his skin was pale--like hers. She wiggled to the top of the water and flashed her tail his direction. Maybe he'd look at her and she could whisper sweet words to him. She liked what she'd seen so far. As she was about to jump out of the water in joy, the form of the black cat materialized dangerously close. Gazing her direction, it moved with determination, stopping short of the river's edge. She felt the animal's disappointment as the dark figure slinked away.

Wiggling free of the rock confines, Trickle caught the current back to her home.

*A talk with Chrissy is in store...and soon.* She shivered with excitement. It had been quite a while since she'd walked on dry land. *I wonder if I'll remember how?*

# Chapter Twelve

Bram and Silas trudged down the back road toward Bram's home. Silas had listened as Bram snorted and snored for the last two miles. Being just as tired as the gnome, the noise was grating on his tender ears.

"Bram. Bram. BRAM!" When yelling at his friend didn't work, Silas resorted to the old fashioned way of alerting and barked his high-pitched yap.

"Wha...what!" Bram yanked his head off his chest, whipping it from side to side. "Why did you bark?"

Silas plunked down. "Because we're at your house and yelling didn't work."

Bram stretched his arms above his head then rubbed his eyes. He lumbered from the cart and trudged to his front door.

"BRAM!"

"What, Silas?" Bram's voice took on a dangerous edge.

"Unhook me."

"Oh--yeah." He sloughed back to the cart.

The terrier rolled his eyes and huffed his impatience at his friend's negligence.

"My apologies, Silas. I can't remember when I've had so much mead and heard so many tales."

"I hope it was worth it because my pads are blistered. Think I'll go home and stay off my paws for a couple days." The terrier waited while Bram unhooked the harness and rubbed the chaffed spots on Silas' fur.

"Rest, my friend. We earned this payment."

Silas limped off and disappeared in the tall grass of the meadow.

Bram watched him go.

"Funny, I've never seen his home." He shrugged his shoulders. "I'm sure he'll invite me one day. Now to a soft bed after a good meal." He pushed open the door to his home. Holding up his hand, he fended off a barrage of questions from his wife.

"Enough. I'll give you a detailed account of my journey after I've eaten and slept in my bed."

Igrayne narrowed her moss green eyes his direction. "Don't hush me. You take off for a week then stagger into my home reeking of mead and road dirt and tell me not to ask questions? If you want a home cooked meal, Mr., do it yourself."

Igrayne stomped into the bedroom, slamming the door behind her.

Bram blew out a deep, weary breath. It wasn't in his nature to argue, and he was bone tired. Tapping gently on the door, he acquiesced.

"I promise I will tell you all of the travails if you will honor me with a bowl of your marvelous stew, my love."

The door squeaked open an inch. "Really? All the things that happened?"

This time he held the hand to his chest. "I give my oath."

She pulled the door open and strode into the living room. "In that case, I'll warm the pot." She padded to the kitchen and lit the stove. Turning to ask Bram a question, she noted the empty room. She retraced her steps through the living area to the bedroom and found her husband planted in the middle of the bed on his stomach, snoring loudly.

"I guess I'll wait until the morrow for those details." She closed the door and turned off the stove. In the front room she picked up her embroidery to pass the time until he woke up or she fell asleep--whichever came first.

~ * ~

Uther was feeling a restless sensation wash over him. Being so long in one place was not in his nature. He gazed longingly down the lane, jumping when the gentle voice spoke in his right ear.

"You don't have to stay."

He turned toward the light smell of fresh meadow grass. "No, I don't but I wish to. I've many years on the roads wandering the land. It's time I settled and shed my nomad ways."

Linda moved to the railing of the porch on Uther's left side. "I think you'll be very unhappy and restless. You are very much the rolling stone, Uther."

He turned to look down on her. "Don't you want my company? I'll depart if you wish me to."

Time slowed as he watched her face mirror the thoughts roaming through her mind. First, she was terrified then hurt by his statement.

"I'm sorry. Did I offend you?"

"No."

He watched her face morph into a calm façade. Her stormy gray eyes took on a flinty hue and shuttered to the outside world.

"I simply meant once a man has traveled extensively, settling in a small community will kill his spirit. That's what happened to my Donald. Oh, they called it cancer, but he was never the same after we put down roots here. Eventually, the stagnation, as he called it, took his life."

Uther placed his hand on the small of her back, his fingers sensing the tightness through her chambray shirt. "I am truly sorry for your loss. Your Donald must have been quite a man to have captured your attention and love for so many years."

Linda felt her breath catch in her throat. Tears were pushing to escape her eyes. She pulled in a deep breath.

"He was very…special. I'm afraid I wasn't able to fulfill his dying wish to remarry. There just wasn't anyone I cared to spend time with," she turned eyes Uther's direction, "until now. I find myself hesitant to share my feelings. Being left alone and lonely is something I've already experienced and don't wish to do again."

Uther turned her to face him. "I *choose* to stay here. I made the decision long ago not to couple when I saw how miserable my brother,

Aethel, was. He married the daughter of the clan chief, a beautiful ethereal creature with flowing silver hair and ocean blue eyes. Unfortunately, she had the heart of an iceberg. It was almost a blessing when she died in childbirth with the second child, a son.

"He met the love of his life in the heat of battle. She was as opposite as his wife was like him; a gnome." Uther chuckled. "She was spunky, talented with a blade and took no foolishness from my brother. He was so smitten with her that…"

Uther hesitated knowing the information he was about to impart was privy to very few.

"…they produced a child."

Linda's eyes popped open. "Wow. The idea boggles the mind. The child must've been very--odd looking."

"No. I don't think he ever learned of the child. By the time his love was deep into the throws of pregnancy, Aethel was bound by his family's word to marry his night elf mate.

"So, you see, Linda," he tucked his finger beneath her chin to raise her face to his. "My family has a history of breaking the norm. When my eyes beheld you for the first time, I knew if I stayed I'd not ever leave."

She reached up and ran her hand down his face, hesitating lightly on his dimpled chin.

"Yet, here you stand." She rose up on her tiptoes, slipping her hand around his neck and pulling him to her. "Stop me anytime."

Uther groaned. "My lady, I would be a fool."

He lowered his head and allowed their lips to meld together. His heart pounded so hard he felt the pressure in his ears and realized other parts of his anatomy were responding in kind.

Linda pressed her body against Uther. She wasn't sure if the pounding she felt in her chest was her heart or his. He'd slipped his arms completely around her and drew her as close to him as possible. She sensed his passion against her stomach, momentarily confused by the pressure. *It's been too many years.* Sensations lost to time began to surge through her limbs, and she allowed them to overcome her.

The lovers pulled back to stare at each other.

"I never had this much emotion for another being. I fought it, believe me. That's why I left before. I couldn't face feeling the kind of loss Aethel did. I saw love tear him apart. Yet, I had to return when I heard my niece and nephew were being so vocal about the loss of their magic. I know them. When they start talking, it isn't too long before they put actions to their words. I…"

Linda pressed her finger to his lips. She stepped back and gently took his hand in hers, leading him inside the Lending Library to the door of her room.

She opened the entry and gave him a quizzical look. "Join me?"

Uther looked into the warmly decorated interior. A smile started to spread on his face.

"Yes."

The two passed the threshold into the Librarian's private sanctum. When the door closed, both knew the life they'd experienced before this day was about to change.

# Chapter Thirteen

Trickle tugged at the piece of magically sealed paper. The time had come for her to get her feet on dry land. For the last three days, the handsome night elf Chrissy had called Morgan appeared on the bank in some very odd clothing. He threw line in the water, but there wasn't any bait or even a hook on the end. She watched him pace back and forth. Around the same time every day, he'd back away from the bank and disappear. She noted the librarian appear on the bank under the tree about the time the night elf would vanish.

Dragging the paper with her, Trickle cruised up stream several oak trees from the library before exiting the water. The oak roots created a cove on the bank where she could make the change from water creature to land creature. Maintaining her small size until she was done dressing, Trickle entered her land home beneath the oak. Beneath a tangle of moss covered roots sat a small dressing table fashioned by the fae workmen, a piece of mirror hung above. The two drawer sides held the slab of wood Trickle used to hold her brush and comb. She set the paper against the wall to dry as she looked beneath the cot for the valise and her clothing.

"Ahh, there you are." Pulling the brown case out, Trickle sat on the rug-covered floor and popped the latches. She ran her hands over the clothes inside before lifting out the top item. The simple, long-sleeved shirt was deep green with white mother-of-pearl buttons. The next item was a pair of fitted black jeans. She pulled the rest of the clothing from the valise and laid them across the small bed. Closing her eyes she murmured words learned during her childhood. The material wrinkled then straightened, all evidence of being locked away for several years gone.

Noting sunlight outside her tree, Trickle opted to take a nap until the sun left the sky for the day. Tonight was the beginning of her hunt for the night elf called, Morgan. The less magic she used to locate him the better. While the two cursed night elves may not have their own magic, she was sure they'd be able to spot the use of magic better than humans.

Grabbing a blanket of moss, Trickle covered her legs, drifting into a dreamless slumber.

*Cold. So cold. Teeth chattering. Cold.* Daring to open one eye, the merfae felt panic grip her throat. *Where am I? This doesn't look like my stream.* Feeling the panic creep up her spine, Trickle magicked a low yellow light orb sending it to the middle of the room. She clutched the moss blanket to her chin as she surveyed her surroundings. Slowly the terror subsided as she realized she was in the oak tree she called home when she walked. The cold continued to plague her so she conjured a heat orb to warm the room. The area outside the tree was dark and she heard crickets starting their nightly concert.

"Time to start my quest to find my night elf." Humming as she moved about, Trickle put together an outfit from her valise she felt would gather attention her direction. She brushed her golden locks one hundred strokes as her mother had instructed and fetched a cape of silken spider's web. A quick glance at the figure in the mirror and she headed toward the opening of her home. At the doorway, she turned to extinguish the light orb catching sight of the paper.

"Almost forgot." She returned to the dressing table to retrieve the item. She hurried to the door, closing then uttering a covering spell to camouflage the tree.

Trickle pulled in a deep breath as she stepped away from the base of the oak. Pulling a perfect pearl from her pocket, she held the smooth pebble in her hand and started to chant:

"Size is but an illusion,
Make this small form,
Become the human norm,

To create confusion,
And bring me the solution I seek."

The air wavered and a glow began at the base of the oak. A rainbow colored cloud plumed up and drifted across the stream. From the center of the light and color display stepped a tall, willowy blonde clad in figure flattering dark jeans. The tailored man's shirt was worn with the hem outside the jeans, collar opened at the neck and flipped up in the back. A black patent belt emphasized the tiny waist of the ethereal creature. The belt matched black, patent three-inch heels the blonde carried in one hand; the other hand carried a matching clutch bag carrying the driver's license she'd tended so carefully. As of this moment, Trickle was now Katherine Lee from Springfield, Oregon. She wasn't sure why this particular piece of paper was so magical, but in previous outings, it had opened all kinds of doors.

Trickle--Katherine closed her eyes and imagined the most likely location she would find her target. With a snap of her fingers, she disappeared.

Appearing at the side of the building, Katherine put on her shoes and flipped her hair behind her shoulder. A quick smoothing of the shirt, and she walked to the sidewalk and up the steps to the gathering place for humans and those who enjoyed their company. She opened the door and was hit with the pulsing of bass guitars thumping out a bottom line to a rock and roll song.

"This is for the fae and Librarian." There was a change since the last time she'd walked on two legs. This was one of their drinking places, but the air wasn't choking with cigarette smoke. She could actually breathe!

"I really need to get out more often."

"No kidding, babe. Let me buy you a drink."

Katherine shrank from the leering, weaving man leaning against the bar. She hurried past him and headed for a booth in the rear of the room. She slid into the leather bench seat facing the door. If the night elf showed, she'd have an eye on him first.

The hours ticked away with Katherine keeping a watchful eye on the door. Her sixth sense had never failed her before. *Why now?* As her patience wore thin and the bar emptied of patrons, she decided she'd made a huge mistake trusting her instincts. She grabbed the clutch and scooted to the end of the bench seat when the door opened and there he stood.

His hair took on the blue hue of the beer sign over the door.

Trickle, Katherine, noted his shoulders were slumped forward and he shuffled to the bar. According to her cousin Chrissy, this night elf was supposed to be so full of himself no one could bear to be near him. He'd left a trail of broken promises throughout the valley. The being she was looking at certainly didn't reek of confidence, quite the opposite. This might prove easier than she'd been lead to believe. A quick thought and she scented her skin with night musk. Plucking up her determination, Katherine stood and walked to the bar a couple chairs from the night elf. She caught sight of him in the mirror at the back of the bar. It was indeed the handsome face she'd been studying from beneath the surface of the stream.

She raised a hand to get the attention of the bartender. "Excuse me?"

The dark haired young man smiled and sauntered her direction. "Yeah, beautiful. What can I do for you?"

Trickle watched hazel eyes take stock of her. She started to speak and stopped. Enchanting someone was on her agenda but not this someone. She graced him with a smile.

"Yes. I've been waiting for a friend and," she shrugged her shoulders, "it looks as if I've been stood up. Can you tell me how to get transportation to Golden Meadows?"

"Wow. You're quite a way from there. It's too late for the buses to run and, truth be told, the cost to take a taxi is exorbitant. You'd be best to stay at one of the local motels and take the bus tomorrow."

Katherine did her best to look disappointed. "Okay. Can I get a cup of coffee and the phone book?" She glanced toward the morose figure occupying the bar stool to her left. The air around him wavered oppressively. His waist length silver hair was confined to a braid down his back. Pulling in a deep breath for courage, she turned to face him.

"Excuse me, but would you know of a nearby motel? I'm new to the area and it appears I've been stood up."

Listless blue eyes stared at her for a moment. Trickle saw the effect of her voice beginning to work on the night elf. The gray tint of his skin receded, and she noted vitality appear in his light orbs.

"What? I'm sorry. I didn't hear you." He motioned to the large black speakers overhead. "Too much noise. Could you repeat that?"

*Got you.* "Just wondering if you were familiar with the area."

The man turned to face her. Animation appeared in his actions and, relaxing his posture, he graced her with a brilliant smile.

*Whew! He's good looking when he smiles.*

"I'd love to help but I'm an infrequent visitor…"

Katherine caught the bartender rolling his eyes in her peripheral vision.

"…so I'm afraid my knowledge is limited. However, if you'd like a ride…I can offer to take you anywhere you'd like in my vehicle."

She graced him with a shy smile. "Thank you for the kind offer, but I make it a policy not to get in vehicles with strangers."

The fair-haired man feigned hurt, clutching his chest and swooning with his other hand to his forehead.

Katherine giggled. "You, sir, are a drama queen."

A flicker of…something dark passed over his face.

"Too true, my lady, but I'm fun to be with, and if you'll allow me but an hour to make your acquaintance, I can promise you an entertaining time."

She thought for a moment and checked the clock at the back of the bar.

"You have one hour to change my mind."

She had him. By the time the hour was up, he'd had her laughing and blushing. She made sure she departed at the time set--one hour later. Stepping around the corner of the building, Trickle removed her shoes and snapped her fingers, picturing the front door of her oak home.

She removed the door spell to enter her dry retreat. As she neared the cot, clothing fell to the ground where she'd peeled it off. Tomorrow she'd magick the items from the floor and clean them. Right now, all she could think of was sleeping. She flopped on the cot.

"I've hooked him." *He wants to meet in a few days. I'll have to use all my tricks to reel him in. We'll just see who wins this fishing contest.*

Yawning, she closed her eyes. All scheming was shelved as the merfae tumbled to sleep.

## Chapter Fourteen

Morgan stood in front of the window gazing on the valley below. A smile curled the corners of his mouth. He couldn't help it. The lady he'd met the night before at the pub made him feel the way he had before he'd lost his magic.

"What are you grinning at, you fool? You should be getting ready to go to the stream bank." Gitty stood next to him at the window. "Good heavens. You have on cologne. You'd better not be planning on leaving me in the lurch."

"I'm not, your highness. Don't get your panties in a bunch. I decided to shower and put on cologne. So what?"

"So, fishermen don't wear cologne." Gitty narrowed her eyes and leveled them his direction. "You've got a new girlfriend."

"What?"

"You have a new girlfriend. We can't deter from our plan. Dump her. When you have a girlfriend, you're absolutely useless."

Morgan faced Gitty. "I don't have a new girlfriend. I felt like cleaning up and putting on cologne. Why is it necessary for me to continue this charade of being a fisherman? We've established the librarian comes out every nice day around two-thirty pm. She takes a quick nap then heads back to the Library. How many more days do I have to waste my time?"

Morgan watched the color of Gitty's face slowly turn to crimson.

"Until I tell you to stop!" She punched his shoulder and stomped to the kitchen.

As Morgan sat rubbing his shoulder, his mind wandered to the previous evening. The mysterious blonde entranced him. In the hour he was given, he'd pulled out his best stories and tamed his boasting. For some reason, he really wanted this enigma to like him for himself.

"I think I succeeded, but she disappeared so fast I won't know for sure."

"Won't know what for sure?" Gitty carried a bottle of water in one hand and a glass container full of some white powder in the other.

"Nothing."

"Right. I've considered what you said, and I think you're on the mark."

Morgan jerked around.

"What?"

"Okay, little brother. I'm only going to repeat this once. You are right. Let's move forward. I've decided today is the day we'll complete our plan. You'll go to the stream as you have for the last few days with Lancelot at your side. When the librarian relaxes to take her nap, Lancelot will let me know and I'll subdue her. You'll need to have your horse ready to receive her. Bring mine as well, because I'll be taking us to a safe location to stash her."

Morgan gawked at her.

"Did you think this was a joke?" Gitty was in his face, eyes wide, teeth clenched.

He leaned back, putting distance between he and his angry sister. "N...no but I didn't think this would happen so soon." *I have unfinished business I wanted to complete tonight.*

"It is. Your impatience gave me the push I needed to move our situation closer to the resolution we want. It's time to act instead of waiting or talking."

Gitty shoved past him toward the back door. "Grab your stuff. We're leaving."

Morgan sloughed to the kitchen to rinse his cup.

"NOW!"

He trotted to his room and grabbed the fishing gear he used as camouflage.

"MORGAN!"

*Good Lord, she's pushy.* "ON MY WAY."

Double-timing his pace, Morgan snatched his sunglasses and bolted to the back door. The pair readied the horses and took off in a flurry of hoofs.

Silence punctuated the ride to the stream behind the Lending Library. Morgan set up in the spot he'd been all week with Lancelot hovered in the closest bushes swishing his tale back and forth. Morgan could feel Gitty's eyes burning a hole through his back. Sweat trickled down his back as the sun beat on his fishing vest. *Damn hot for spring.* Movement across the stream caught his attention.

The Librarian had a book in hand this time and settled in the sunspot verses the shade. She opened the text, turning to a specific page and started to read. Five minutes passed before the book teetered from her hands and rested on her legs. Morgan tensed. Things were about to get bad.

Lancelot let out a low growl. *Time?*

Morgan pulled the line from the water and made as if to button up his fishing. "Yes. She's sleeping."

The large cat trotted back to Gitty. An apparent conversation ensued between feline and night elf. Morgan heard the scuffle of hooves and turned to see Gitty walking her stallion away from the bank.

*Maybe she's changed her mind.*

Lancelot trotted up to Morgan. *Mistress says you are to follow her and be ready to follow her orders.*

"Great." Morgan set his fishing gear under a tree and mounted his steed. There was no turning back now.

*Follow me.*

He kept his eyes on the waving black tail pointing straight up in the air until they stood next to the slumbering Librarian. Gitty dismounted and pulled the water and white powder from her saddlebags.

"What are you doing?" Morgan whispered.

"Shut up and watch. This will guarantee cooperation and no damage to her."

Gitty scattered a bit of white powder on a washcloth she'd previously packed in the bag. She then sprinkled water droplets on the powder. White smoke start to spiral but quickly dissipated. She placed the cloth over the nose and mouth of the Librarian. In less than a minute, the form on the ground was limp. A fact Gitty proved by picking up and dropping the Librarian's arm to the ground.

"Get your butt over here and pick her up." Her voice was dangerous and low.

Morgan dismounted his horse and moved to the supine figure on the ground. He slid his hands beneath her shoulders and knees, lifting her from the grass. She was surprisingly light, barely one hundred pounds. His next stop was to slip her on his saddle before mounting up. The form leaned back against him and he noted the compactness of the woman.

Gitty swung up to her saddle and wretched the reins to the right.

"Follow me. Don't ask questions and don't lose me."

"I thought you were going to take her on your horse." Morgan's eyes narrowed at his sister.

"Things change. Just try to keep up and don't ask stupid questions."

Morgan nodded. When Gitty was this brusque, any deviation from what she said could bring dire consequences. The odd traveling companions galloped around the open meadows, keeping to the wooded areas away from prying eyes. Gitty stopped to let the horse drink from the upper section of the stream before plunging the riders into the forest on the opposite side of the valley.

For two hours they rode through wooded acreage. When the Librarian would start stirring, Gitty would repeat the process of putting the white powder on the washcloth, adding water then placing over the librarian's face.

Just when Morgan thought they must be getting near Eastern Oregon, Gitty slowed the pace of the ride.

"Stay here." She slipped off her horse and vanished into a dark copse of pines.

Morgan sat on the fidgeting horse that started pulling up tufts of stray grass nearby. Gitty emerged from the woods and waved him over.

"Don't go any further until I get my horse." She jogged to where she'd left her stallion and swung up to the saddle. "Follow me."

The pines closed around the small caravan as they moved deeper into the woods. Light beamed through the canopy of pine boughs. Five minutes into the ride, Morgan noted an area ahead where the forest thinned to expose a cabin. Gitty dismounted her horse and tied the reins at the porch railing. She motioned Morgan over. He nudged his mount forward.

Gitty lifted her hands. "Give her to me."

Morgan slid the sleeping form off the horse with ease.

"Tie up your horse then help me secure her."

Morgan did as he was bid, ducking his head under the doorway as he entered the shelter.

"When did you find this?"

Gitty dumped the limp form on a couch facing the stone fireplace. "I built it."

"What?"

She turned to find his eyebrows raised and shock on his face. "Don't look so surprised. I'm quite handy with a hammer and nails."

"I--I have no doubt. I just don't remember you being gone long enough to do this."

"Well, I was. Can we make sure she's securely fastened so we don't have to worry if we go outside?"

He moved to her side and assisted as she bound the Librarian's hands together at the wrists and feet at the ankles.

"You going to put something over her mouth?"

Gitty looked at the prone figure. "No. She can yell all she wants. No one will hear her. We're too far from civilization. I'm going to put a blanket on her so she doesn't get too cold."

"That's rather kind of you."

Gitty turned to him. "Not really. She's no good to us dead."

Morgan nodded his agreement.

His sister rummaged through the closet nearest the front door and brought out a battery powered camp lantern. "Use this until I get back. I'm going to locate dinner. Don't let her talk you into anything. Right?"

"Right."

Gitty shut the front door behind her. She'd planned this to the last detail but didn't want Morgan to know. He was the loose cannon in this formula. Who knows what he would blurt out given enough alcohol? She rode the quarter mile to the storage barn she'd constructed to house food supplies. Dismounting Glade, she pulled a set of keys from her vest pocket. Finding the appropriate key, she inserted it into the lock and turned. The lock opened easily and once removed, the door was easy to slide. Gitty stepped into the interior and stood still for a moment, adjusting her eyes to the darkened interior. Her breath caught in her throat as the light from the opened door featured an etched, wood portrait of Glade, the male night elf and love of her life, in a shadow box she'd created. She'd commissioned a member of his clan to create the likeness for her. Next to the portrait were his forest green, leather hauberk and broken blade. He was gone but not forgotten. Gitty's heart ached.

"Who knows my love? I may join you soon."

She went about the business of gathering supplies to feed three for a week. The food wasn't exotic but would keep them alive. After loading the supplies on her horse, she locked the door and headed back to the cabin.

Morgan walked around the large room. He was having a difficult time imagining his sister sawing wood, banging nails, installing windows or anything related to building. The sofa faced a stone fireplace complete with mantel. Framing the hearth was wood and stone shelving and two small windows, one on either side. The hardwood floor was a deep red brown in color and emitted a warm glow adding to the cozy feel of the room. To the right of the room, Gitty had installed a half wall that divided the sleeping area from the sitting area. Opposite the fireplace was a galley style kitchen with the fundamentals, nothing more. A bathroom had been built off the sleeping area. All in all, Morgan had to agree, this was an amazing retreat.

In his reverie Morgan failed to notice the librarian sit up. She groaned.

"Oh, my head. Where am I?"

He jumped. "What?"

"You! What have you done to me? HELP! HELP!" Linda tried to stand, only to fall forward and cut her lip.

"Great! See what you've done now?" Morgan grabbed the woman and hoisted her up, plopping her on the couch. "Sit still. You can yell as loud as you want. Hell, you can yell until you're hoarse but no one will hear."

Linda glared at him with blood running down her lips. "You're Morgan Saun, aren't you?"

"Lady, be quiet. It doesn't matter who I am. You can try to get away if you want but trust me, the effort will be futile. I'm getting a cloth and some Band-Aids to stop your lip from bleeding." He strode to the bathroom and opened the medicine cabinet door. An unopened box of the adhesives sat to the right. Grabbing a clean washcloth, he ran cool water over it and snatched the bandages from their spot in the cabinet.

Linda ran to the front door, both hands on the handle, trying her best to open the barrier. Her face dropped in surprise as the door opened and she stood facing Gitty.

"I should have known. You."

Gitty sneered at her. "Yeah. Me. You and your merry little band of fae friends ruined my life with your stunt of taking my magic. It's been nearly a year, and I think it's time I got back to being myself again. Don't you?" She pushed Linda back to the couch without consideration of her captive's stumbling. "I have no love lost for you, Librarian." Gitty leaned over to look at Linda's face. "What the hell happened here? Morgan!"

He bolted from the back of the cabin carrying bandages and a washcloth. "What?"

"What did you do? She's bleeding."

"Yes, I know. She tried to get up from the couch, tripped and fell." He sat next to Linda and placing his fingers either side of her head, turned her to face him. Linda fought to break free of his grasp.

He dropped his head to his chest. "Please. I really don't want to hurt you."

"Right. That's why you have me trussed up in some god forsaken hut in the middle of nowhere." Linda's eyes radiated hate his direction.

Gitty leaned down level with Linda. "Let me tell you something, Other. Morgan here is a lily livered coward who happens to be very adept with a blade. He's happiest carousing with you mortals in some pub, trying to impress the women. He probably wouldn't hurt you.

"Me, on the other hand, I have no love for the human population as a whole. As I'm going to live to be two hundred fifty years old or older, I'm more than willing to cut you to pieces to get my point across to the people I need to convince. I'm the one you need to fear."

Backing away, Gitty spoke to Morgan. "Fix her up. I'll put something together to eat in the meantime. I don't want her dead--yet." She turned a glare Linda's direction.

Linda shrunk back and looked at Morgan. He shrugged his shoulders.

"She means it. Now, please let me clean up your lip and put a bandage on it." He put the cloth to her face and very gently cleansed the blood from her lip. Once he dried the spot, a bandage was applied. Morgan checked his handiwork and rose from the couch.

Gitty was slamming pots and pans on the stove and grumbling. "I didn't sign on for this. All I wanted was a simple snatch and grab with a compliant body. Who the hell knew this *old* Other would have such-- spunk? I don't need this."

Morgan waited until she quit ranting. "I have an idea."

Gitty whipped around with a large spoon in hand. "Great." She shook the spoon as she spoke. "This was your idea in the first place. What now? Let her go free?"

Morgan stepped backward with each shake of the spoon until he felt the couch back hit his thighs. He gingerly took the spoon from his sister. "Let's go outside. Turn off the stove and let's take a minute."

Gitty tossed a look Linda's direction. "What about her?"

"Use your sleeping potion."

She crossed to the counter and grabbed the cloth, sprinkling crystals and adding water. As she came at Linda, her captive tried to wiggle away. Winning the battle, Gitty had her prisoner unconscious within a few seconds.

"We may have to tie her to a chair. Let's go." She nodded toward the front porch.

When the brother and sister stepped on the precisely crafted boards of the front porch, they opted to leave the door open.

"Okay, what's your bright idea now?" Gitty placed the cloth over the porch railing and crossed her arms.

Morgan held up the washcloth smeared with blood. "What was going to be your next move? You're heading up this production."

She leaned against the support. "A note saying she's being held until the council convenes and agrees to reinstitute our magic--one hundred percent."

"How far do you think that will get you?" Morgan lifted a brow.

"As far as I need it. I don't think Uther will be happy about his lady love being held captive."

"True. But all he'll do is employ his magic to locate our whereabouts and come rescue her."

"So you have some idea that will inhibit this ability?"

Morgan smirked and held up the washcloth. "This."

Gitty huffed disbelief. "Get real. How's a bloody washcloth going to stop Uther from using his magic?"

"By seeing the bloody cloth, he'll know we're serious. There's enough blood to make him question how bad his lady is hurt. We can suggest if he tries anything, she'll be returned in pieces. How do you think he'll react to that?"

She stood looking at her brother. A smile slowly began to turn up the corners of her lips.

"I was beginning to wonder if our mother had been fooling around with the stable boy before you were born. That is a truly *wicked*, devious plan. I love it!" She unfolded her arms and headed for the cabin, humming a Celtic victory song.

Morgan smiled. Finally. His sister was actually appreciative of his plan. He'd have to remember this day; they came so seldom.

Entering the building, Morgan went to the kitchen to search for a storage bag. He dropped the bloodied cloth inside and sealed it. Rummaging in a small desk placed against the wall, he located paper and a pen. He sat at the two-person table and created the ransom note.

*We have the Librarian. If you want her back alive and in one piece, send your reply via the Mouse Network to the family warehouse in Springfield for further instructions.*

"Gitty, what do you think?"

She read the two-line note and nodded. "Excellent. For once, I can say I couldn't do better myself. How will we get it from the warehouse?"

Morgan chuckled. "That's the best thing about the Mouse Network."

Gitty raised an eyebrow. "What?"

"They have no loyalties. Given enough payment, they'll go anywhere to deliver a message. I've been working with one particular messenger who'll go pretty much where I ask."

"Well, well. Aren't you the devious one?" Gitty stood. "Can you contact your messenger and tell him to meet me at the house with the response?"

"WHAT?"

"Yes, little brother. You get to baby-sit the hostage."

"Great." Morgan grumbled.

"Just remember, when this is all over and you have your magic back, you'll thank me. I know if that--Other--tried anything with me, I'd have no problem eliminating her."

"Fine. But I have a...date in a couple days."

"If all goes well, you'll be able to charm her and get lucky with your magic." Gitty smirked. "I should be home in about an hour. Have your messenger meet me there in two hours."

"How am I supposed to do that since you have tied me to this house?"

Gitty glowered at him. "Get a messenger to find your messenger."

"How?"

"That's your problem not mine."

Morgan grumbled and watched his sister leave on her horse.

"Open my big mouth and wind up babysitting. Some day…"

# Chapter Fifteen

Uther checked her room. He walked the path to the stream and checked her favorite spot along the bank, finding her book opened to her favorite poem but no other sign of Linda. He trotted back to the Lending Library and hunted until he found Chrissy.

"Have you seen Linda?"

The tiny nymph smiled and looked at him, a twinkle in her eye. "Lost your lady love?"

Uther felt the blush crawl up his cheeks. "I'm serious. I've looked all over the property, and I can't find her. She's not in the garden or on the stream bank. I even looked in her room to be sure she wasn't napping. I'm worried. She didn't say anything to me about running an errand."

"Well, you know she's been alone for a long time. I don't think she would tell you if she was running an errand." The nymph cocked her head from side to side looking at her layout for the May Day festival. "Do you think I could put the gnomes next to the meadow fae?"

Uther looked at the seating chart. "Probably not. Why not put the mountain fae next to the gnomes? They get along better. I keep forgetting how independent Linda is. I mean, she doesn't always tell you if she's running an errand, does she?"

Chrissy had been erasing and rewriting when Uther's question struck her.

"Actually, she tells me where she's going every time she leaves." She turned to him, her brows knit together. "Uther? We need to do another search. It's not like her to take off unannounced."

May Day plans set aside, the odd pair decided to split the property

85

in half and mounted a search. Uther took the building and front of the property; Chrissy opted to fly around the garden and stream. Her ulterior motive was to talk with Trickle and see if her cousin had any pertinent information.

Chrissy buzzed to the stream. *Trickle, you here?* Three tries yielded no results. Chrissy gave up trying to contact her cousin. It was obvious Trickle wasn't home. She checked with the birds and talked to the rabbits and no one had seen Trickle for a couple days. Chrissy hovered above the water and murmured. "Where are you, cousin?"

The garden proved as elusive as the stream; no sign of Trickle or the Librarian. Chrissy was feeling ineffectual and frustrated as she returned to the Library.

By the look on his face, Uther had met the same fate.

"Any luck, Uther?"

"No. I checked everywhere I could think of and no Linda. You?"

"Nothing. What are we to do? Call in the local police?"

"No. Other's police are very uncaring and will suggest she left of her own accord. I don't believe it. Do you?"

Chrissy shook her head. "No. She loves this place too much to just walk away. There's something going on."

Uther nodded his agreement. "Yes, and I can guess who's behind it. I'm afraid we'll have to wait until they make the next move."

Chrissy's wings quavered. "Uther, I'm afraid."

"I am too, my little friend, I am too."

The next morning Uther sat at a table near the kitchen, grasping a cup of Chrissy's Killer Coffee. His bloodshot eyes told the tale of his previous night. As he forced the dark brown liquid down his throat, a mouse wearing the maroon vest of the Mouse Network approached him.

"I'm looking for an Uther."

The night elf narrowed his eyes to focus on the messenger.

"You have found him."

"Please sir, a message for you is in the pocket upon my back. I'm to wait for a reply."

The mouse turned his body so Uther could retrieve the paper tucked within the vest.

Chrissy winged in from the kitchen and hovered over Uther's left shoulder. She watched him withdraw a bag with a note taped to the front.

Uther pulled the paper from the bag and sucked in a deep breath when he spotted crimson blotches upon a white item inside. He unfolded the paper and read the cryptic message. Opening the baggie, he withdrew the contents; a washcloth covered in blood. Uther uttered an ancient curse.

Chrissy dropped to the table and reached out a tiny hand to touch the washcloth. "Please tell me this isn't the librarian, Uther."

"I can't, my little friend. The beings we're dealing with have no soul or conscious when it comes to the lives of others."

The nymph yanked her hand back and broke into sobs, winging her way to the kitchen.

Uther got up to locate pen and paper. When he found what he needed, he sat at the table and put together a carefully worded reply.

*If you value your life, you'll not harm a hair on the Librarian's head. What do you want?*

He tucked the reply in the vest of the mouse. "What is the cost?"

"None, sir. It has been prepaid."

He watched the gray creature scamper from the room and out the front door.

It took all his power not to follow the creature. He toyed with the idea of placing a magic tracker on the mouse but knew his adversaries while unable to *use* magic, would be able to spot the magic tracker.

"There has to be a way." Pacing the center aisle of the library, he examined his memory for other times when magic couldn't be used to track a foe. "Why can't I think of…hawks! If I can only remember the spell to call them." Uther stopped his motion and furrowed his brow. His hand rested on a book on the shelves. Eyes shut tightly to recall the proper incantation, he would get close to remembering then feel the thought slip away. He opened his eyes and turned to gaze at the spine of the book where he'd placed his hand. ***The Forgotten Spells of Merlin.*** *Can it really be that easy?*

Retrieving the tome from its neighbors, Uther flipped to the page for aviary spells, sliding his finger down the page to the words used for summoning messenger birds. The moment he saw the ancient words, his sudden amnesia evaporated. *Of course.*

He replaced the work on the shelf, which he noted was filled with volumes on magical creatures and spells. Rolling the words around his head, he moved as quickly as his feet would allow to the lane in front of the Lending Library. The sky was dotted with rain clouds in various hues of gray, the sun peeking from behind them. He whispered the words to the chant twice, as recommended, and waited for results.

The air shirred with the languid flapping of powerful wings. Uther looked to the sky. His gaze was captured by the white and tan chest of an American Kestral floating on the thermals toward him. Once the creature leveled out, Uther watched as it flew at him back winging to rest comfortably on his shoulder.

*Did you call for me, night elf?*

Uther was surprised at the throaty, deep tone of the bird's voice. "I did."

*How can I be of assistance?*

"I need eyes and ears to find something I've lost."

*Why not look yourself?*

"Because I'm not quite sure where it is. I received a message from one of the Mouse Network representatives and need to see where the creature finally ends up. Are you familiar with them?"

*Yes. We're forbidden to eat them. Waste of good food, if you ask me.*

"This one left within the last fifteen minutes and is probably heading East."

*Can you be sure?*

"No, but I know the author of the original message and how devious her thinking is. If you don't find the messenger within the day, don't concern yourself with the hunt. Come back here and we'll agree on a price."

*Fair enough. I'll return within twenty-five hours either way.*

"Fly safely and don't get caught."

*I'll watch my back.*

Uther watched the kestral take flight on the spiral winds soaring toward the clouds.

*I've done all I can--for the moment.*

He watched Chrissy buzz around the Lending Library, putting together plans for May Day and envied her distraction. Waiting was the enemy here, and he knew if he didn't find something to occupy his mind and hands, he'd go crazy.

Chrissy whizzed past him.

"I'm going for a walk, if anyone is interested." Uther exited the building to the porch. The walls inside felt as though they were closing in on him. He pulled in a deep breath of the rain-tainted, spring air and made his way to the entry road. Maybe a walkabout would clear his mind and freshen his perspective. The driveway was lined with tulips and daffodils boldly opening their petals to greet the new season. He marveled at the serenity of the landscape. If he could just stand in the lane and inhale all the spring smells for the rest of his life, he'd be a happy man. At this time, his world was about to implode and he felt powerless to find a simple solution.

A reverberation in the distance caught his attention. Uther stopped and concentrated. He realized the noise was moving toward him at a fast pace. *It's coming this way but not to the Lending Library.* He zeroed in to the direction of the sound. Narrowing his eyes, he trained them to a road situated next to the farmer's field a quarter mile to the east. The tap tapping from afar morphed into thundering hoof beats. Uther beaded in on the figure of a familiar form racing a finely muscled black horse across the valley. The she elf sat ramrod straight on the stallion's back, her white hair billowing behind her as the animal galloped to their destination.

*Gitty. Where are you going in such a hurry?* He tried to touch her mind but met a blank barrier. *So, you're either blocking me or have lost your ability to telepath.*

The hurried horse and rider continued their journey up the road to the mansion on the hill.

Uther closed his eyes and mentally searched the area for the other night elf. His mind touched many creatures busily preparing for summer but couldn't sense Morgan. *That's odd.* Since the two night elf siblings had been deprived of their magic, word was if you spotted Gitty, Morgan was close by. *She's in a hurry and he's nowhere to be found. Unfortunately, I believe my fear has been realized. The Saun family is, once again, right in the middle of trouble.*

~ * ~

Linda smelled food. Her stomach grumbled. She couldn't remember the last time she'd eaten. Slowly, she opened her eyes and panicked. Nothing looked familiar. Where was she? She tried to bring her hands up to rub her eyes but couldn't budge them. Her throat constricted as she tried to swallow. Out of the corner of her eye she caught a quick flash of white and involuntarily emitted a low groan.

*Where am I? What's happening and why is my head pounding?*

"Where…?"

The question hung in the air. Linda realized her voice was nothing more than a whisper. She tried to get her legs to move but met resistance. Frustration hampered her actions. She cleared her throat with difficulty.

"Where am I?" That seemed to catch the attention of the other body in the room.

"Let me tell you where you aren't…at home."

Morgan appeared within her range of vision and she groaned out loud.

"I was hoping this was just a bad dream."

The night elf sneered. "Lady, when you play with the big boys, you suffer big boy consequences. If you're new *friend* values your life at all, you'll be going home."

"I don't know what you're talking about."

"Right. We'll play that game if you insist."

Linda tried to sit upright. "Please. Can you help me to sit up?"

Morgan's brow furrowed. "If I have to…" He moved to the bed and righted the librarian.

"May I sit on the couch?"

Morgan rolled his eyes. "Look, lady, I've got an important function to attend and babysitting you is not what I planned. I'll put you on the couch if you promise not to try to escape. I'm not as heartless as my…partner but I'll have no hesitation to duct tape you to the bed."

"I promise I won't try to escape. I'd put up my hand but…" Linda shrugged. "…at the moment my hands are unavailable."

Morgan slipped his hands beneath her shoulders and knees. He lifted her from the bed and within two steps had her upright on the couch. "There. Now be quiet."

"Thank you." Linda closed her eyes and slowed her breathing. She knew if she were to have her wits about her, she needed to try and eliminate the pain in her head as much as she could.

"Here." Morgan placed a bowl filled with macaroni and cheese next to her. "I'm going to undo your hands, but if you try anything, well, I'll have to take measures."

"I'm too hungry to do anything but eat."

"Good." Morgan stepped behind the couch and untied the ropes binding her hands.

Linda rubbed her wrists to push blood to her fingers. When the tingling and pain started, she knew she wouldn't lose any digits. Grasping the bowl in her fingers, she noted the lack of utensils.

"I need something to eat with."

"Fine."

She could hear him moving around the kitchen and jumped when a spoon was shoved in her face.

"Remember, I have no compunction about knocking you out."

"So noted."

Linda dug into the pasta, reveling in the taste of cheese and macaroni. *Never thought mac and cheese would taste so good.* She took in the layout of the cabin over the top of the bowl: *bathroom behind the bed in the right corner of the building, fireplace in front of the couch, kitchen behind and, most importantly, door to freedom on the left.* For the moment, compliance was the best course of action, but there would come a time in the near future where she *would* escape. When she did, this night elf better watch out. Her Donald had taught her a few self-defense moves from his time in the service. He'd always worried about them being so far from town. She hadn't practiced in a while, but the body had memory that would come in handy.

Morgan watched her devour the food. When she finished, he took the bowl and spoon to the sink. "I'll feed her but I'm not about to do woman's work."

Linda tucked her upper lip between her teeth to keep from smiling. This he night elf was in a foul mood, and she wasn't yet ready to push him to the brink.

"How long are you keeping me here?"

Morgan knelt in front of the hearth trying to figure out how to start a fire. He jumped when she spoke.

"As long as it takes to get what we need."

"I see."

"No, you don't. You've never had magic, and wouldn't have a clue how much it adds to being alive. Not having my magic has been...pure hell." He rose from his knees and stomped out to the porch.

*I've hit a nerve.* This time Linda let a smile touch her lips. *I have ammunition now. Bad move, night elf.*

# Chapter Sixteen

Trickle--Katherine--stretched her arms above her head. She smiled as she crawled out of bed. The he night elf, Morgan, really wasn't that bad. To top it off, he was very good looking. It had been quite a while since she'd indulged herself with a mate. The human ones, while easy to enchant, had such frail bodies. They aged so quickly and couldn't hold up their part of the deal. She'd hated to do it, but the last one she had, she wiped his memory and left him at a hospital. Sad. He was an especially nice man who doted on her. Oh, well.

This he night elf could live quite a bit longer. Katherine loved that idea.

"I'm hungry." The one thing she hated about this form was the need to constantly feed it. She couldn't afford to waste the time doing the shopping thing so she'd magic the body into thinking it was full.

"I'm going back tonight to see if he's there. I've made up my mind I want this man for myself. I know Chrissy won't object because he'll do anything I ask--when I enchant him."

She hummed as she tidied up her land home. She'd need to present a picture of domestic perfection to her object of desire before weaving the spell to make him hers forever. Tonight was going to be the most exciting time she'd had in quite a while.

~ * ~

Chrissy hummed around the Library, adding touches here, moving furniture there. She was expecting a large turnout for the May Day celebration and all had to be in order. When she'd sent Bram and Silas out to warn the locals about the night elves, she'd sent invitations to the May Day celebration with the Sky Network. Surprisingly, they'd returned with responses from nearly all the clans in the valley and the forests. If everyone showed, the local Others were sure to notice.

"Tough. We were here first. They'll just need to adjust." She flew through the coffee shop and out the door to the porch. Uther had taken up camp on the wooden appendage and was currently snoozing in one of the chairs. She hated to wake him, but while he slept, a carrier from the Mouse Network had arrived with another message for him.

"Uther?"

She was greeted with a grunt.

"Uther. UTHER!"

"What!" He jumped upright from his reclining position.

The wood nymph hovered before his eyes clutching a large white envelope. "Please take this. It's getting heavy."

He reached for the envelope, the white paper container dropping to the deck when the nymph could no longer hold on.

Uther leaned down and picked up the packet. His name was scrawled across the front in a familiar hand. He placed it in his lap and stared at the paper.

"Aren't you going to open it?" Chrissy winged to his leg and landed. She reached out a finger and touched the packet. "Do you think it's poison?"

Uther sighed. "No, little one. I don't think it's poison, but I believe it carries bad news."

She crossed her arms and tapped a tiny foot on his leg. "Uther. I've seen you face a field of opponents and charge in with no regard for your own life. How can one piece of paper cause you such hesitation?"

"Because on the battlefield, I only had to concern myself with the safety of my troops and myself. Most of my men I'd known from childhood and knew of their bravery and selflessness. This, I know, concerns someone I…" He gazed at the tiny creature before him showing more courage than he felt. "...I love for the first time in my life. I never knew how much she would affect my feelings. What if they've killed her, Chrissy? How could I go on?"

Chrissy unfolded her arms and winged to his face. She laid a small hand on his cheek.

"You'll go on because you know Librarian wouldn't have it any other way. She is nothing if not brave. After all, she did stand up to Morgan and Gitty."

"Which is why we're in this bind now."

"Open the envelope, Uther."

Fingers quavering, he tore open the sealed packet. Inside was a fine linen slip of paper, which he retrieved and unfolded.

Chrissy watched his face turn crimson as he read. She winged away from the chair and waited. Uther crumpled the paper and threw it on the wooden deck.

"I knew it! I knew they'd never sit quietly and accept what they'd done to themselves."

He stomped from the porch. Chrissy watched him disappear around the side of the house. She magicked the crumpled paper and read the contents.

*We have one demand:*

*Call all the clans together and reinstate our magic--in whole.*

*If you don't comply in the next 48 hours, we'll start sending the librarian back to you: one piece at a time. Send your reply via the Mouse Network to the family warehouse in Springfield.*

*G & M*

Chrissy buzzed to the side of the house to see if she could spot Uther. He sat in the librarian's favorite spot on the stream bank. She raced to his side.

"Uther?" She kept arm's length away in case he was too angry to think.

"Yes?"

"What are we to do?"

"I don't know, Chrissy. I can't afford to have Linda killed because she stood up to those two, yet giving them back their magic would bring nothing but trouble to the valley and the clans. Gitty would make life hell on all who crossed her."

Chrissy moved closer to him and settled on a stump near him. "She acts as though she is the gift to this valley. I've never seen anyone so self-involved. Well, maybe Morgan, but considering he's her brother, it's to be expected."

The two sat morosely for a moment. Chrissy watched pain flash across his face then noted a change of his body. He sat up straight and his eyes lit up.

"That's it!" Uther turned to the nymph. "You, my dear, are a genius."

"Okay, but what did I say that makes me a genius?"

"Vanity."

"Yeah. The two of them have it by the boatloads."

He turned and gazed at her. "Are you willing to help me free Librarian?"

She humphed. "How could you doubt that?"

"I'll need you to lend some of your magic to me."

"Done. What are you going to do?"

"Give Gitty something to think about. Morgan seems to have adjusted to life in the Others' world but Gitty fancies herself above all of us. Are you ready?"

Chrissy nodded and moved opposite him.

He sat straight up and closed his eyes. Chrissy hovered and closed her eyes.

"Please put all of your concentration on my incantation.

*Gitty,*

*Every minute as a prisoner she spends,*
*Brings you one moment closer to your end,*
*The vigor and vitality you so crave will soon disappear*
*Replaced by the horror of old age and death you fear.*

*Your life source will find its way*
*To one whose life you would betray*
*Be forewarned*
*The change begins this very day.*

As he'd been taught, Uther uttered the spell three times, lying back on the soft grass when the chant was ended.

"There's your answer, Gitty Saun. I hope you enjoy it."

Chrissy fluttered to the ground next to him. "Whew! That should knock her socks off."

"I hope so."

"Is there any way to reverse it?" Chrissy saw him smile.

"Yes. But the cost of reversing the spell is to accept what she wants changed. I seriously doubt she'll understand the simplicity of it. No, I think we're going to see a change in the she-night elf and a change in our own Librarian."

Chrissy seemed revived. She flew in front of Uther and winged loop-de-loops. "Yeah. We get to see what Librarian looked like when she was young." She stopped and looked directly at him. "Will it last?"

Uther sat up on his elbows. "As long as she lives which, now with Gitty's life source, will be quite a bit longer than she expected."

"I have things I need to get done for May Day. Do you want me to make you something to eat?"

"No. You've done more than enough for me today. Thank you." Uther watched the wood nymph fly off toward the Lending Library. He plucked a long piece of grass and stuck it between his teeth. The spell would either put an end to this foolishness or backfire to cause a war no one could win.

He desperately hoped the former would happen. Very shortly, time would tell.

# Chapter Seventeen

Gitty stood beneath the warm flow of water and allowed the tension to be swept away with the dirt. She'd sent the second letter laying out their demands. By this time next week, she'd be back in control of her life and have the magic that was rightfully hers.

Turning the water off, she stepped to the rug and buffed her body with the towel until she glowed pink.

"I think my first move will be to bulldoze that miserable hovel, the Lending Library. Then I'll ban Uther from ever coming back to these parts and, in a generous display of compassion, allow the renegade fae the ability to go back to the homeland. Let's see how well they manage on the Emerald Isles."

She chuckled and retired to her room to change into her comfortable jeans and a sweatshirt. Warm slippers on her feet completed her outfit and she meandered to the living room. She was restless but didn't want to read, so she pulled out her Tarot cards and decided to give herself a reading. If she were correct, all signs would point to success. Gitty shuffled the deck and placed the first card on the coffee table.

"What? This can't be!"

~ * ~

Morgan combed his hair for the final time. Looking in the mirror, he smiled at the reflection. "Showtime. Tonight, I'll win--without magic." He winked and entered the living area of the cabin.

The librarian was settled on the couch, watching his preparation with interest.

"Date?"

He glared at her. "None of your business. However because I'm going out, you get to stay on the bed." He picked her up and carried her to the cot, securing her ropes to the head rail and foot rail of the bed.

"What if I have to use the bathroom?"

He turned to her. "Hold it or wet your bed. I don't care. I've been here for the last forty-eight hours, and I have something important to do. I told Gitty I was attending to business tonight and I will. I'll leave the light on for you, but otherwise…you are on your own. See you tomorrow."

He headed for the door.

"HEY! You can't just leave me here."

The corner of Morgan's left lip raised slightly. "Yes I can and I am. Deal with it." He started out the door and turned back. "You can yell as loud as you like. There's no one around for miles. Goodnight."

The door slammed, leaving Linda alone. *This is not good. What the heck am I supposed to do?* She figured if nothing else, she'd just sleep. Lately, her energy levels seemed to be dropping. *Must be age.* She tried closing her eyes, but they kept popping open. *What is wrong with me?*

In frustration she tugged at her bindings. She felt them give. *What?* She tugged again and felt the rope move. Normally, she would have been short of breath and feeling the need for a nap, but at this moment, Linda felt strength in her arms she'd not experienced in years.

The night elves perception of her as a weak Other was working to her advantage at the moment. Morgan had tied the ropes with a great deal of slack, expecting her neither to fight nor to be able to yank them loose.

Excitement fueled her. She jerked the ropes and popped to a sitting position. The bindings on her wrists had been tied with no thought of them being undone. Linda slipped her hands through the loops and massaged her chaffed, raw appendages. She needed to hurry, however. If either Morgan or Gitty returned and found her out of her bindings, they'd tie her so tight she could lose a limb.

The ropes on her feet proved more of a challenge, but Linda's energy seemed to be endless. She looked at her fingers in awe. The last few years had proved to be a lesson in frustration, with rheumatory arthritis invading her hands and knees and making everyday tasks impossible. She felt no pain whatsoever.

"I'm not sure what's going on but I'll take it." Linda swung her legs over the edge of the bed. Her feet tingled. She was forced to sit and twist her feet around until the circulation returned. Testing a foot on the floor, she was relieved to find her appendages functional and able to propel her away from the cabin.

Linda scavenged the drawers in the small cottage. She found some energy bars and a flashlight. She tucked the bars into her pockets and flicked the switch of the flashlight, blinking when she got light. In a drawer in the kitchen, she located extra batteries she cached in another pocket.

The librarian padded to the entrance and opened the front door slowly. Twilight blanketed the forest, giving the trees and surrounding plants an eerie glow. She slipped her body out and closed the door behind her. In front of the cabin was a single lane, disappearing into the canopy of trees. Linda bolted down the stairs and began to run. She might not have much energy, but she was going to use what she had to expedite her escape. But how to get back to the Lending Library?

"Moss grows on the north side of the tree." All those years in Girl Scouts had given her a bit of forest knowledge. When the lane ended in another road, Linda felt desperation creeping in to her mind.

"No. I'll not give up so soon." She stopped and pulled in a deep breath. When she opened her eyes, she noted horse prints headed in one direction. She looked to the sky and mouthed "Thank you" before proceeding to follow the tracks.

Three hours passed before the forest thinned and the Librarian began to recognize landmarks. She was amazed at her stamina and reasoned it must be the fear of being caught again. The meadow opened up, and she could make out a few lights on buildings close to her home. Now was the time she needed to be especially careful. Just another half mile or so and she'd be in her own home. Linda stopped and pulled in a deep breath.

"It's now or never." She bolted across the meadow, keeping her eyes on the lights of the Lending Library. She stumbled on to the driveway and began to cry. Nearing the porch, she saw a figure in the chair and hesitated. Did she continue forward or try to camouflage her arrival by going around back?

"I'm too tired to circumvent coming in the front. To heck with it." Linda pulled herself tall and walked to the porch, taking the steps confidently. She turned to face the figure on her deck.

Uther had kept an eye on the movement he'd noticed in the meadow. Someone was crossing the fields rather late at night. He trained his eye on the lone figure moving intently in his direction. When the figure started up the driveway, Uther tried his best to identify the person but was having a difficult time. The figure hesitated just out of the range of the porch light. It moved up the stairs and turned to face him, shoulders squared.

"LINDA!" Uther jumped from his chair.

Linda thought she would faint from relief. She'd recognized the long, white hair and angular limbs as that of a night elf, but her recent experience had wiped away any recollection of the night elf who cared deeply for her.

"Oh my god, Uther." Linda pushed out an exhausted breath. "I'm so glad it's you." She stood stiffly, checking the face coming toward her. "It is you, isn't it?"

He wrapped his arms around her and pulled her to his body. He buried his face in her hair and pulled in the essence that was Linda. "Yes, my lady, it is I. And I'm relieved, delighted and a million other things to see you."

Linda wrapped her arms around him and immersed herself in his strength. For the moment, all was well.

# Chapter Eighteen

Morgan arrived at the pub and took his usual seat. He looked around but couldn't locate Katherine. His stomach dropped. "She's not here." He nodded at the bartender. "The usual, please."

The man pulled a glass from the cooler and filled it with draft beer. "Three dollars, Mr. Saun." Morgan reached for his wallet.

"I've got this. Please get me a blended Pina Colada. Thank you."

Morgan started and twisted to stare into the blue green eyes of Katherine.

"Did you think I wasn't coming?" She graced him with a shy smile.

"I, uh, I wasn't sure." He gave her a lopsided grin.

Katherine let him hang for a moment. "I couldn't wait to come back so I took a little--longer--to get ready. I hope you don't mind?" She twirled around.

Morgan took in the vision. "Not at all."

"Good. Now, where were we when we parted ways?" She looked directly into his eyes as she spoke.

Morgan saw her mouth move, but all he could hear was the sound of the ocean. *This is the most beautiful woman in the world. I don't ever want to leave her.*

Trickle watched his eyes glaze over. *You're mine now...forever.*

~ * ~

Gitty waited impatiently for her brother to show. "Where is that idiot?"

She moved to rise from the couch and caught her breath as pain shot through her hands and knees. *What the hell is happening?* Sucking in a deep breath, she pushed off the divan.

*Must be because I haven't done enough riding lately.*

A quick trip to the bathroom to get an aspirin would take care of the pain issue. Gitty made her way down the hall, halting to catch her breath every ten or so steps. *This is ridiculous.*

She flipped on the light and opened the medicine cabinet. The aspirin bottle proved to be a challenge to open. Her fingers didn't seem to want to work the way they should. When she finally got two tablets out, she turned on the cold water and filled the glass. Tossing the pills down her throat, she washed them away with a big gulp of water and closed the door to the medicine cabinet. That's when she realized something was horribly wrong.

The face staring back at her was...showing signs of age. Skin sagged at the neck and chin line. The surface of the face was dry and gray looking. There were tiny lines around the eyes and mouth and in her platinum hair were--gray--hairs.

Gitty stepped back and opened her mouth. A blood-curdling scream rent the air. The last thing she remembered was some old woman looking at her from her bathroom mirror.

~ * ~

Linda stepped inside the door and pulled in a deep breath. The smell of her books always settled her nerves.

"Are you hungry, my lady?" Uther gently swept her hand into his.

She turned to him, marveling at the adoration shining from his eyes. "I'm so hungry I could eat a complete cow tonight. I guess it was all that running."

Uther's eyebrows raised and his eyes popped open. "You ran here?"

Linda nodded. "Yeah, and it's really weird because I'm not tired at all. I know it's going to irritate Chrissy, but I want to fix my own dinner.

How about you, Uther? You hungry?"

She thought his smile looked a bit odd.

"No, my lady. Just out of curiosity, have you looked in a mirror lately?"

"Uh, no. I was too busy running for my life. I must look a fright."

He chuckled. "No. I'll let you see what I'm talking about."

Linda barreled to the kitchen and found the room empty. "Good. No interlopers in my kitchen." She pulled pots and pans from various cupboards and rummaged in the refrigerator. Not finding much food with girth, Linda opted for an omelet. When she'd mixed the ingredients and put them on two plates, she carried the food to the dining table inside the Library.

Uther had taken a chair and waited until she quit fussing to try and carry on a conversation. He touched her hand and looked up into the steel blue eyes. "Stop fussing. Sit and enjoy the meal. We need to have a serious discussion but not over this marvelous omelet."

She felt the color rise to her cheeks. "As you wish, sir."

Silence filled the room as the two indulged their taste buds in the veggie omelet. When Uther had finished, he dabbed his mouth with a napkin, placing it over the plate.

"I received a ransom note from Morgan and Gitty yesterday threatening to send you back in pieces if I didn't gather the clans and return their magic."

Linda coughed into her napkin. "What? Are you serious?"

"Very."

"I hope you didn't do anything foolish, because I couldn't live with it if you gave up something for me."

Uther's sly smile put Linda on guard.

"No, I didn't do anything foolish; well, not too foolish. I remembered an incantation my mother taught me to use on vain people who needed to be gently reminded to stop their self centered ways."

Linda leaned back in her chair and crossed her arms. "What did you do, Uther?"

He squirmed in his chair. "Put a reverse aging spell on her."

"That doesn't sound too bad. Why are you being so evasive?"

"Linda? Go look in the mirror." He nudged her with his foot. "Go."

Linda was looking for the opportunity to wash up from her dusty day walk. She entered her bathroom and put the washcloth in the sink to dampen. Then she looked in the mirror and passed out.

~ * ~

Uther had suspected the shock might be too much, so he'd quietly followed her and was there to catch her when she dropped.

"Who, how, what?"

He put his finger to her lips. "I put a spell on Gitty; for each minute she held you captive, she would age and you would, well, unage. I'm guessing you're about thirty-five right now."

Linda's hand went first to her hair. "It's black again. I'd forgotten how dark it was." She then ran her fingers around her eyes and mouth. "The lines are gone."

She pushed off the floor and grasped the sink, looking at the face of the person she'd been thirty years earlier. "Oh my. I'm not sure what I think. I'd gotten used to the old face."

"Do you want me to change it back?"

"Oh, hell no." Linda lifted her blouse to view the young, taut stomach she'd forgotten she once possessed. "I think I like this." Her eyes twinkled a deep blue.

"We need to talk, my lady." Uther took her hand and led her to the porch where they sat in chairs next to each other.

"What's so important?" Linda stuck her hands in front of her to admire the taut skin and lack of age spots.

"I want you to be my life companion."

Linda dropped her hands and faced Uther. "Are you serious?"

"More serious than I've been about anything in my life."

"When?"

"How about we have the clan chieftains approve it at the May Day celebration?"

She took a moment and examined her nails. "I wasn't sure I wanted to ever spend time with anyone after Donald, but…" she looked at Uther. "…you're not anyone; you're special. Yes. I'd love to spend my forever with you."

Uther leaned over and captured her lips under his. His heart pounded in his chest and he felt a stirring in his loins. *Later.*

# Chapter Nineteen

May Day

The yard was a patchwork explosion of flowers celebrating the spring. A pole had been erected in the front yard for the young fae to participate in the ringing of the Maypole. Chrissy winged her way back and forth directing the activities and sporting a new outfit for the occasion.

Linda gazed at the profusion of colors highlighting her library.

"I never thought I'd see the day when all of the clans would, again, come together in my home and celebrate."

Uther snugged her close to his side. "They have a special place in their hearts for you, my lady. You accomplished that which no Other has done. Come to think of it, no fae has been able to get all these ruffians to agree."

Linda smiled as she laid her head against his muscled chest. "Who would believe I could be so lucky twice in my life?"

Uther placed a gentle kiss on the top of her head. "It's I who is the lucky one to find you."

The fae children ran and winged their way through the Lending Library and on to the deck; the pounding of little feet reminding the grownups of a simpler time.

Bram and Silas sat in the chairs designated for them as co-heads of the May Day celebration. They were attended by their children and watched their wives talk about babies and childcare issues. Bram's wife was the local midwife who would be attending Silas' Mrs.

When the sun reached its zenith in the sky, each chieftain solemnly marched to the center of the front yard near the Maypole. They stood, waiting for the din of the crowd to lessen. When their presence didn't sufficiently lower the clatter, Kayne, the current clan chieftain of the meadow fae, put his two front fingers in his mouth and whistled. The shrill explosion stopped all the noise in the meadow.

"Thank you." He dipped his head in appreciation. "We have gathered today to join in the celebration of new life. For many of us..." he winked at Ailidh, heavy with child. "...this year brings bundles of joy. For others, the end of a threat we've all dreaded has been achieved. It's for this reason we are happy to join with our friend and ally, Uther, night elf, and Linda, Librarian and Other.

"At this time, they've chosen to join their houses together. A mighty spell has brought Linda into our folds and she now bonds with the fae. Will Uther and Linda please join us up front?"

Linda, her long, dark hair braided down the center of her back wearing a tan floor length dress with flowing lace sleeves and Uther, dressed in his finest tan leather pants and jerkin held hands as they walked to the center of the yard to face the chieftains.

Kayne flashed a grin at the pair and cleared his throat.

"Are all the clans represented?"

A roar of "AYE!" rang through the air.

"Does any here denounce or disagree with this pairing?"

"NAY!"

"Then let it be known that Linda, the librarian and Uther, the night elf, shall be joined together until the breath is gone from one or both of them."

The crowd erupted in raucous cheering and Uther bent to his lady, lifting her from her feet and kissing her.

The musicians struck up a wedding jig and the newly twined couple danced until they were breathless.

Bram leaned over to Silas. "What happened to the other night elves?"

Silas raised his head from his paws. "Rumor has it the male got himself tangled up with a merfae and is residing in the stream out back. As far as the she night elf...seems she hasn't left her hilltop home since the librarian was found. Some say she's withered away to dust. Long as she stays away from me, I don't care."

Bram tapped his pipe against the chair. "I agree."

A comfortable silence descended between the friends.

Joining cake cut and devoured, presents given and the newly attached couple on their way to some time alone, Chrissy finally settled in her lounge chair and fanned herself with a leaf.

"Who would have thought we'd ever see the pairing of a night elf and an Other? Guess our librarian was always about defying the odds."

# About the Author

C. L. Kraemer has been a gypsy all her life. From her military child beginnings to her might-not-get-this-chance-again attitude after she left home, she's seen most of the continental United States as well as Hawaii and Alaska. She hopes to travel the world but is content to stay close to her family in the Northwest in Oregon—for the moment.

Three contemporary romance novels written under the nom de plume, Celia Cooper, **Old Enough to Know Better; Sun in Sagittarius, Moon in Mazatlan,** and **If Only** were gifts from the writing gods. A fourth novel, **Cats in the Cradle of Civilization**, release date December 2008, written as C. L. Kraemer is her first venture into the mystery genre. *Wings ePress, Inc.* has been the publisher of these four offerings.

**Healthy Homicide,** the October 2008 launch book for a new publishing house, *RoguePhoenixPress*, picks up the torch again in the mystery world. In February 2010, she contributed to two Valentine's Anthologies at *RoguePhoenixPress*: **A Valentine Anthology**, with a story titled, ***Lending Library***, and **A Different Kind of Valentine** with a story titled, ***The Prize***.

She has completed the base story for a Dragon Fantasy series, **Dragons Among Us**, which was released August 2010 by *Rogue Phoenix Press*.

***Meadows of Gold*** is another faerie story released in *RoguePhoenixPress'* March 2011's anthology, **A St. Patrick's Day Tale**. A third story featuring the Fae of the valley outside Eugene, Oregon will be available in the **May Day Anthology** set to come out in mid-April or the beginning of May 2013. This tale is entitled, ***Defying the Odds***.

The second in the dragon series, **Dragon Among the Eagles**, became available for public reading in June 2011.

August 2011 saw the release of **Shattered Tomorrows**, a Mystery/crime novel loosely based on the May 7, 1981 shooting at the Oregon Museum Tavern in Salem, Oregon where four lost their lives and twenty were wounded.

A motorcycle poker run is featured in her March 2013 release, **Joker's Wild** and the third in the dragon series, **Dragons Among the Ice**, to be released in 2013.

For detailed information, visit her Web sites for background on her books

www.celiacooper.com
www.clkraemer.com

*Defying the Odds*
was originally published by Rogue Phoenix Press
as part of the *a May Day Anthology*
by Chrsitine Young, C. L. Kraemer, Rosemary Indra, and Genie Gabriel

May Day has been celebrated since Roman times with dancing, baskets of flowers, and bonfires. In this collection of May Day stories, Rogue's Angels--Christine Young, C.L. Kraemer, Rosemary Indra and Genie Gabriel--continue the celebration with humor, faeries and falling in love.

Highland Miracle -- Christine Young

HURTLED THROUGH TIME, Sean Michael Sterling, landed in the midst of a May Day celebration he didn't understand, assuming the role of Laird Sterling.
ILLIGITAMATE CHILD OF NOBILITY, Reagan Douglas searches for a way out of her half brother's house.


Defying the Odds -- C.L. Kraemer

The night elves on the hill aren't happy without their magic. They concoct a plan to punish those who were involved in the act that rendered them almost human. Meanwhile, Uther, the rogue night elf, has returned to woo the Librarian to be his eternal mate.

Love in Bloom -- Rosemary Indra

When childhood friends reunite it takes two fairies and a matchmaking daughter to help them admit their true love for each other.


No More Poodle Skirts -- Genie Gabriel

After drifting for years in the innocent age of the 1950s, a woman struggles to join today's world by finding a career and a new love, with some help from her zany family.

Other books by Christie L. Kraemer
Available at Rogue Phoenix Press

*Healthy Homicide*

Two murders have occurred at the Barrel Springs Day Spa. Police hurry to find the method and reason before anyone else is murdered.

MANIC READER REVIEWS says: Healthy Homicide by C.L. Kraemer is an intriguing plot driven mystery. The plot is well written and pretty much carries the whole story...

*Dragons Among Us*

In a world full of anomalies such as the platypus and self reproducing Komodo dragon, is the human race willing to accept that dragons may be real?

Sapien Draconi-human-dragon shape shifters-all over the world face this dilemma every day. The question has become life and death as their species is plagued with unexpected and unwanted shifting in the most unlikely of places.

The Ancient Ones-full-blooded dragons-can offer advice, but few seem to put forward workable solutions to the problem.

The fate of the shape shifters hangs in the balance, and an answer must be found before the Homo Sapiens find, dissect, and hunt Sapien Draconi to extinction.

## Dragons Among The Eagles

Aleda Sable faces the toughest decision of her life--to stay in dragon form, live as a two-legged or put one foot in the human world and one talon in the dragon world.

An urgent call from her newspaper editor sends Aleda to report on an accident whose driver appears to be a dragon. Authorities have the scene locked down and aren't allowing access to anyone. Television broadcasts flash pictures of scaly legs hanging from a crashed car. However, the bodies disappear into thin air. When the stations try follow-up reports, all they find are state highway workers busily tearing up the roads.

In determining the truth of the shifter disappearances, Aleda finds the truth of her own dilemma.

## Shattered Tomorrows

Lucy Daniels has a secret--a deeply guarded secret.

Her life was going along just fine until she accompanied her best friend, Cassie, to her attorney's suite on top of the Equitable Building in downtown Salem, Oregon.

Once inside the lawyer's office, the world turned upside down and Lucy was forced to face a demon from her past. Thirty years ago, life had been different. Lucy had discovered Prince Charming and was headed to her happily ever after.

That's when the devil intervened and because of her brush with the devil, innocent people died.

## Joker's Wild

Four brothers raised in the Northwest.

Two choose to stay and pursue life in Oregon. Two are seduced by the promise of Hollywood.

Life throws the Palmer brothers an ugly curve when two are killed in preventable accidents. Even more upsetting is the lack of justice in the trials of the perpetrators.

The remaining brothers will find justice using a shared passion of all the participants--motorcycle poker runs.

# C. L. Kraemer
is also featured in these anthologies available at
Rogue Phoenix Press

*A Different Kind of Valentine*

A collection of four short stories:

*Witness* by k. J. Dahlen

When Colten finds an injured woman the police are looking for her, should he trust his own judgement about keeping her hidden from the law even if it means she might kill him?

*The Prize* by C. L. Kraemer

A computer geek learns valuable life lessons when he is given his dream car as well as a condo and the perfect job.

*Crazy 'bout You* by Clay Renick

Can a psychologist and a romance writer find true love in time for Valentines                                                                          Day?

*Time Changes* by Nicolette Zamora

Laurie is just about ready to give up on love when she spies Rob Hender, her high school sweethearts older brother.

## A St. Patrick's Day Tale
by
Christine Young, C. L. Kraemer, Genene Valleau

Tumble through time…

…to Ireland in 1817, when tensions are high between Protestants and Chatolics and faey people guide the fate of villagers. A lovely Catholic lass stumbles upon the weakly ritual fisticuffing between Irish lads. She falls into the lap of a handsome young Protestant. Family ties, grudges, and two conniving faeries threaten their budding love. But the faeries outsmart themselves when they hijack a time machine that has mysteriously appeared in their forest and are whisked to…

…Eugene, Oregon in the 20th century, amid a property feud between the local faeries and night elves. The conniving faeries from Olde Ireland try to stir up more mischief. However, a warrior gnome convinces the magic folk to control their own destiny, and forces the intruding faeries to take refuge in the time machine again, spinning their way toward…

…A modern day castle in western Oregon. An eccentric inventor is determined to reclaim his wayward time machine and save his beloved wife from her latest misadventure. If only they can travel safely past the black hole…

## A Valentine's Anthology

*The Lending Library*-a fantasy by C. L. Kraemer

Faeries try to fit into the human world when the forest where they make their home is destroyed by a mysterious enemy.

*Chasing Rainbows*-a contemporary romance by Genene Valleau

An eccentric aunt, an inventive uncle, a mother who wears poodle skirts, and a brother who wears pearls provide a hilarious backdrop for the courtship of a young woman who yearns for a "normal" family.

*The Gift*-an historical romance by Christine Young

A man and a woman on opposite sides of the Civil War get a second chance at love after one final battle returns soldiers to their war-torn homes to rebuild their lives.

*VISIT OUR WEBSITE*
*FOR THE FULL INVENTORY*
*OF QUALITY BOOKS*:
*http://www.roguephoenixpress.com*

# Rogue Phoenix Press

*Representing Excellence in Publishing*

*Quality trade paperbacks and downloads*

*in multiple formats,*

*in genres ranging from historical to contemporary romance, mystery and science fiction.*

*Visit the website then bookmark it.*

*We add new titles each month!*